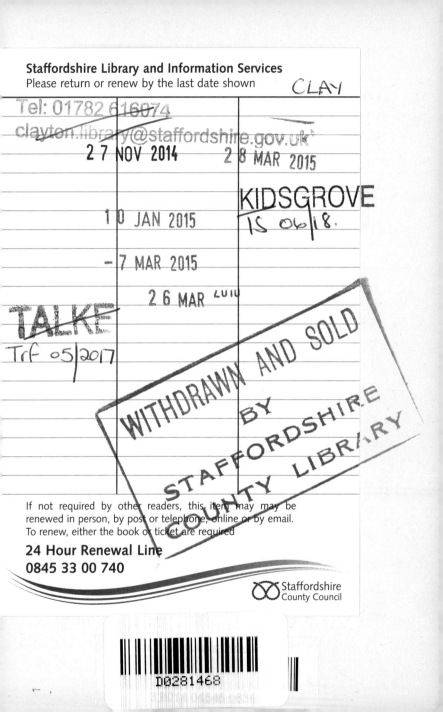

THE CHAINED MAN

When a band of stranded Christmas travellers is forced to spend the night in an isolated local pub called the Chained Man, the last thing they expect is murder in their midst . . . Lattimer Shrive puts his amazing powers of detection and deduction to work to solve three seemingly inexplicable cases . . . And a real murder on national radio proves surprisingly tricky to solve. These five detective stories by Gerald Verner will baffle and entertain in equal measure.

GERALD VERNER

THE CHAINED MAN
AND OTHER STORIES

Complete and Unabridged

LINFORD
Leicester

First published in Great Britain

First Linford Edition
published 2014

A catalogue record for this book is available
from the British Library.

ISBN 978–1–4448–2124–6

Published by
F. A. Thorpe (Publishing)
Anstey, Leicestershire

Set by Words & Graphics Ltd.
Anstey, Leicestershire
Printed and bound in Great Britain by
T. J. International Ltd., Padstow, Cornwall

This book is printed on acid-free paper

The Chained Man

1

Glum and shivering, the little group stood on the snow-covered platform of Moorland Halt and stared in consternation at the solitary railway servant who covered the duties of porter, booking clerk and stationmaster.

'Do you mean to say,' said Trevor Lowe, 'that the nearest hotel is twelve miles away?'

'Ay, mister, I do,' said the man. 'Twelve mile it be, an' you can't stay 'ere because I'm goin' to lock up.' He jerked his head towards the wooden shed at the end of the long platform, which constituted the entire station.

'Well, I think it's disgraceful!' declared an elderly stout-ish man. 'Disgraceful! The railway company have got us into this position, and the railway company should get us out of it!'

'Since they're not likely to,' remarked Lowe, 'we must do something for ourselves.'

The snow was still falling steadily, and to add to their discomfort the wind had risen — an icy, penetrating blast that swept across the open moorland and found its way through the thickest overcoat, chilling them to the marrow. The girl looked blue with cold, her threadbare coat offering little protection against that cutting north-easter.

The dramatist and his secretary, accompanied by Inspector Shadgold, had been on their way to St. Merryan, a little Cornish village nestling in the moors, to spend Christmas with a friend of Lowe's. They had changed at Bodmin from the Western Express to the local train, and were halfway on their journey across country when disaster had overtaken them. A heavy fall of snow from the wall of a cutting had blocked the line and rendered further progress impossible. With their fellow passengers they had decided to walk back along the track to the last station and seek accommodation for the night.

The guard, who had walked back with them, had got on the phone to Bodmin and received orders to remain with his train until the breakdown van arrived.

'Surely there must be some place nearer than twelve miles,' said Lowe irritably.

The porter shook his head impatiently.

'I tell you there ain't!' he answered. 'Only the Chained Man, and you'd best stay out than go there.'

'The Chained Man? What's that?' asked a tall, fair man, watching the shivering girl anxiously.

'It's a pub about a mile away, along the Moor Road,' replied the porter. 'But if you takes my advice — '

'Why, what's the matter with the place?' asked the stout man.

'Well, it's queer,' grunted the porter. 'Joe Cornford — that's the landlord — is a surly brute, and the place ain't got too good a reputation. Nobody in these parts won't go near it. There was a feller killed there five years ago, and since then — '

'Never mind about it bein' queer, mate!' exclaimed the cockney. 'I bet it's a darn sight better than freezing to death on this blinking platform.'

'Oh, well, you please yourself!' said the porter, after a slight hesitation and shrugging his shoulders. 'But I'd rather stay out on the open moor myself than spend a night at the Chained Man. If you come out of the station with me I'll show you the way.'

They followed him to the wooden building that served as booking office and waiting room, waited while he carefully locked up behind him, and then descended a flight of wooden steps to the lower level of the road.

'Follow that there path,' he said, pointing to a ribbon of road that faded away in the curtain of falling snow. 'And don't say I didn't warn yer. You'll find the Chained Man a mile along on the left.'

They had some difficulty in keeping to the road, the thick covering of snow rendering it almost indistinguishable from the surrounding moorland. It seemed that they had walked miles and their feet and hands were numbed with the cold before a faint light ahead on the left of the road warned them that they had almost reached their destination.

As they drew nearer they heard the creaking of a signboard somewhere up in the snow-flecked darkness above them, and presently came upon the post that bore it. Away to their left was a shadowy building; a light gleamed from a first-floor window.

'Thank 'eaven!' said the little cockney fervently who during the walk had confided to all and sundry that his name was Arty Willings. 'Mother's wanderin' boy 'as come 'ome at last!'

Making his way up to the low porch, Trevor Lowe found a rusted knocker and beat a thundering tattoo. There was a long delay, and then the door was pulled open; an unkempt, dirty-looking man holding an oil lamp peered out.

'What is it?' he growled ungraciously. 'What do you want?'

Lowe rapidly explained the situation. The man, whom he took to be Joe Cornford, the landlord, nodded surlily.

'I can put you up,' he said, 'but you'll have to take pot luck. We ain't used to receiving guests 'ere these days.'

'If you can provide us with a fire, something to eat and a decent bed, that's all we want,' retorted Lowe.

'And some beer,' put in Mr. Willings. 'Don't forget that, mate!'

' 'Ow many of you are there?' growled the landlord.

'Ten,' answered the dramatist.

'I've only got eight rooms,' said Cornford, 'but come in an' I'll do what I can.'

They left their various suitcases in the passage and entered the room he indicated: an oblong, low-ceilinged apartment with a fireplace at one end, in which they noticed, thankfully, that a log fire was burning.

'Well, queer or not,' remarked Mr. Willings, warming his hands, 'this is a blinking sight better than bein' out in the perishin' cold, ain't it?'

The stout man, who had confided to Lowe that his name was William Makepiece, heartily agreed with him.

The landlord returned with an armful of logs, and accompanied by a slatternly-looking woman whom he introduced as the 'missus', who said that she would show them the rooms. And unprepossessing enough they were — small, dirty and badly furnished. When they had washed in tepid water, brought them by the landlord, they went back to the coffee-room to find the pleasant smell of fried bacon permeating the atmosphere and the table laid with a mixture of odd crockery.

During the meal that followed, the dramatist took stock of his companions in misfortune. They were a curious mixed lot, he found. There was William Makepiece — middle-aged, grey-haired, and jovial. The little dark-haired, ruddy-faced cockney, Arty Willings. A pale-faced, thin man, who had as yet scarcely opened his lips, and whose name Lowe did not know. The young, fair-haired man, who had introduced himself as Frank Cotton, and who was paying marked attention to the girl. A bald-headed man, whose neatly waxed moustache was of a suspicious blackness. There were also a little meek-faced man called Pilbeam, and the girl.

She interested Lowe more than any of them. The frightened look which he had surprised in her eyes when she had got in the carriage at Bodmin had deepened. He caught her once or twice glancing uneasily at the men grouped round the table. Her eyes flickered from face to face with an anxious, searching look, as though she was trying to satisfy herself about something that was troubling her mind.

When she had finished her meal she rose and with a muttered good night, left them. Gathering round the fire, the rest of the party chatted desultorily until, by tacit consent, they broke up and made their way to their various rooms.

The wind had risen to a gale and was howling round the place, whistling in the chimneys and rattling the windows. Somewhere below, a loose shutter was banging intermittently; and, tired though he was, this sound kept Lowe awake for some time.

2

It seemed to Lowe that he had only been asleep for an instant, when suddenly he was wide awake. At first he thought it was the sound of the loose shutter swinging in the wind that had wakened him; and then, as he listened, he heard the low rumble of voices. They came from somewhere beneath him, and he was on the point of turning over and going to sleep again when he heard somebody scream — a sharp cry of agony that broke off abruptly in the middle!

He sat up in bed, his senses alert; but although he listened, there was now no sound from below. He slipped out of bed and put on his jacket and trousers over his pyjamas and opened the door.

The passage was in pitch darkness, but when he reached the head of the stairs he caught a momentary gleam of light from the hall below.

'Who's there?' he called softly. 'Anything the matter?'

Instantly the light went out, and he heard the creak of a door, but no one answered.

He reached the hall and started to cross it to enter the coffee-room, but suddenly he stumbled and fell over something that lay on the floor. His hands, outstretched to check his fall, came in contact with something silky — silky and wet!

With a muttered exclamation he scrambled to his feet, opened the coffee-room door, and going over to the dying fire kicked one of the logs till it blazed. In the flickering light he examined his hands. They were both darkly stained with something that glistened red in the flame. A glance through the door and he discovered the reason.

Huddled on the floor was the figure of a man clad in pyjamas and dressing-gown. Trevor Lowe went over and bent down. Staring up at him was the distorted face of the stout man, William Makepiece, and round the knife that protruded from the breast of his silk pyjamas was a similar stain to that which covered his hands.

The man was quite dead. One look at the sightless eyes staring up at the discoloured ceiling told him that. And it was murder!

He remembered the voices he had heard immediately on awakening, the sudden flash of light, and the creak of the door. On the end of the long table was the oil lamp which the landlord had brought to the door to admit them. Lowe touched the china shade and drew his fingers away quickly. It was still unpleasantly hot. It must have been that light which he had seen when he called from the head of the stairs, and it must have been the murderer who had blown it out and escaped as Lowe made his way down to the hall.

An uncomfortable little shiver ran down his spine. The man must have been crouching somewhere in the darkness as he had groped his way to the door of the coffee-room . . .

He hurried over to the fireplace, and with a spill, which he made from a strip torn from an old newspaper, lit the oil lamp. Then he bent down over the dead man, placing the lamp on the floor, so that its light shed a pool over the motionless form. The man had been stabbed through the left side of the chest, and the weapon was a large clasp-knife with a horn handle. He saw something white gripped between the fingers: part of a large-sized Christmas card that had been torn across.

As he straightened up, the figure of the

landlord came out of the gloom. He caught his breath as he saw Lowe; and then, as his eyes dropped to the thing on the floor, his coarse mouth fell open and he stared at it, his small eyes wide with horror.

'Did you kill him?' he whispered hoarsely, finding his voice.

'I? No!' snapped the dramatist. 'I was awakened by a scream, and coming down I found him like this.'

'Thunder!' gasped the landlord. 'You're all over blood!'

'I am aware of that,' retorted Lowe quietly. 'I stumbled over the body in the dark.'

'Oh, yer did, did yer?' There was open suspicion in the other's tone.

'Listen!' said Lowe sharply. 'I didn't kill him and I know nothing about him. Now, go upstairs and waken my friends.'

He waited, staring with half-closed eyes at the corpse. Presently he heard the thudding of knuckles on wood, followed by the sound of voices, and a moment or two later Shadgold appeared on the stairs, his eyes heavy with sleep and his bristling hair ruffled.

'What's the matter, Lowe?' he asked;

and then, following the dramatist's eyes: 'My God! What is it, an accident?'

'No,' answered Lowe gravely. 'Murder!'

'Murder!' The ominous word was echoed by Arnold White, Trevor Lowe's secretary, as he peered over the Scotland Yard man's shoulder.

Briefly and concisely Lowe explained.

'We must wake everybody in the house,' said Shadgold, 'and we ought to notify the local police.' He turned to the sullen-faced landlord who was leaning against the door-post. 'Have you got a telephone here?'

Cornford shook his head.

'You say you heard the person, whoever it was, leave the room as you were coming downstairs?' Shadgold went on, rubbing vigorously at his toothbrush moustache.

'I heard somebody moving about,' corrected Lowe. 'Also there is the fact that the lamp had only recently been put out.'

'You don't know anything about this, do you?' Shadgold glared at the landlord.

'What should I know about it?' retorted Cornford. 'There ain't no reason why I should want to kill the feller. I never saw 'im till tonight!'

'What were you doing up?' asked Lowe, noting the momentary hesitation before the landlord replied.

'I couldn't sleep,' he answered, passing his tongue over his dry lips. 'That blessed shutter was making such a row. I came down to see if I couldn't fix it!'

The sound of protesting voices reached them from upstairs, and in the light of the lamp that Shadgold had placed on a table Lowe saw a collection of scantily dressed figures being shepherded down the stairs by White.

'I've wakened everybody,' said the secretary, 'except the girl.'

'I'm afraid you'll have to waken her,' said Lowe. 'We can't make any exceptions!'

'I can't waken her,' said White. 'She isn't there!'

3

'Take me up to the girl's room,' muttered Lowe beneath his breath to his secretary.

White led the way upstairs to the end of a long passage and paused before an open door on the right.

'This is the room,' he said, and Lowe entered the tiny chamber.

It was in pitch darkness, but this was dispelled when Lowe lit the candle. On the floor was the girl's suitcase. It was open and the contents lay strewn in every direction. There was evidence of frantic haste here — haste on the part of somebody, presumably the girl herself. A dark object caught his eye among the crumpled bedclothes — a dark, furry object — and as he straightened out the none-too-clean coverlet, he saw that it was the threadbare coat with the fur collar which she had been wearing.

Moving away from the bed his foot struck something, and bending down to see what it was he found the girl's handbag. It was lying half under the bed and, like the suitcase, had been opened and its contents scattered on the floor.

He collected these and put them on the bed. There was a nearly used-up lip-stick; a flat metal container for face powder; a nail file; a little purse containing a shilling, some coppers, and a pound note; a handkerchief; and a letter — or rather the envelope of a letter — addressed to Iris Lake, 125b, Coram Street, W.C.2.

He noticed that the faded curtain which draped the window had been caught up, where someone in shutting the window had rammed a bit of the hem between the window and the wooden crosspiece. Only a person in a terrible hurry — or panic — would have overlooked that and left it.

He went over to the window and pushed it up as far as it would go. Outside, and barely two feet from the window, was the flat roof of a one-storey extension to the main building. Outlined in white by the snow, several chimney stacks were visible, but what interested him most was the unmistakable tracks of feet in the snow on the rooftop.

It did not take him long to visualize what had happened. Someone had entered the girl's room. Possibly she had been stunned. Then something had alarmed the intruder; he had picked up the senseless girl and carried her out on to the roof and hidden behind the stack until the alarm

16

had passed. He shut the window.

They went downstairs again and found the coffee-room deserted. Shadgold had evidently marshalled the others into the bar.

'We'll take a look outside,' said Lowe, and as he opened the front door a swirling cloud of snow blinded him.

He switched on the torch that he had taken from White's hand and swept the light over the white expanse of snow that seemed to stretch away to infinity in front of the door. The virgin whiteness was undisturbed by mark or footstep.

Fighting their way in the teeth of the howling gale, the driving snow making their cheeks smart and tingle, they made a complete circuit of the old building, and presently found themselves back in the porch from whence they had started. And in every direction all around the inn the thick carpet of snow lay smooth and undisturbed.

'That settles it,' said Lowe, as he opened the door and they thankfully entered the comparative warmth of the hall. 'No one came from outside and no one has left from within.'

'Which means that the girl is some-where on the premises,' said Arnold White, vigorously rubbing his numbed hands.

'Also the murderer of William Make-piece!' added Trevor Lowe gravely.

4

Shadgold appeared at the half-glass door leading into the bar as they came in.

'Hallo!' he grunted. 'Where have you been?'

Lowe explained, wiping the melting snow from his face and neck with his handkerchief.

'H'm!' grunted the Scotland Yard man. 'Then the killer is amongst that bunch I've got in there.'

'Have you succeeded in discovering anything?' asked the dramatist.

Shadgold shook his head gloomily.

'They all swear they were in bed and asleep, and heard nothing until White roused them. And they all deny having known Makepiece or ever having seen him before until they met him on the train.' He rubbed irritably at the back of his coarse neck. 'Of course, somebody's lying,' he grunted, 'but the difficulty is to find out who. Not one of them has got an alibi, except Cornford.'

'What's his alibi?' asked Lowe.

'His wife,' answered the Scotland Yard man. 'If you can call her an alibi. She confirms his story that he came down to see if he could fasten the banging shutter, and that he didn't move from her side until then. She remembers noting the time by the alarm clock they keep in their room, and it was half-past two when Cornford got up.'

'Well, somebody wasn't in bed,' said Lowe. 'Before we go any further I think we ought to find Miss Lake.'

'Who's Miss Lake?' demanded Shadgold, and then: 'Oh, you mean the girl?'

'I feel sure she's in the building,' said the dramatist, and he gave the inspector a brief account of his discoveries.

'It certainly sounds bad,' agreed Shadgold. 'I think you're right, we ought to find out what has become of her.'

It was not until they searched the fourth room on the landing that they were rewarded for their diligence. The cupboard here refused to open when Lowe tried the handle.

'What is it?' grunted Shadgold.

'I can't get this cupboard open,' said the dramatist. 'It's locked. See if you can find anything to break it open with.'

'This'll do,' said Shadgold, handing him a short, rusty iron poker.

Trevor Lowe took it, forced the point between the edge of the cupboard door and the jamb and pressed against it with all his strength. There was a cracking of splintering wood, and then with a loud snap that was like the report of a pistol the lock gave. As it did so the door swung open of its own accord, and something heavy that had been leaning against it fell out with a soft thud at their feet.

It was Iris Lake!

Her ankles and wrists had been tied with cord and a rough gag had been secured about her mouth. She was clad only in a thin suit of pyjamas and her hands and face were blue with cold. On her forehead was an ugly bruise and for a moment Lowe thought she was dead. He lifted the girl up, laid her on the bed, and untied the handkerchief that was tightly bound about her mouth.

She gave a little moan and stirred restlessly, but her eyes remained closed.

With his pocketknife Lowe slashed through the cords at her wrists and ankles. Her hands were like blocks of ice, and he rubbed them vigorously to restore the circulation.

'See if you can get some brandy,' he said sharply.

Presently Shadgold returned with a bottle and a glass, followed by the agitated and indignant Mr. Willings.

' 'Ere, what's all this?' whined the little cockney. 'What d'yer want me up here for?' and then, as his eyes lighted on the figure on the bed: 'Struth! 'Ow did she get 'ere?'

'That's what we're waiting for you to tell us,' said the dramatist harshly.

'Me?' Mr. Willings' voice was even more shrill than usual in his excitement. 'Why ask me? 'Ow should I know?'

'This is your room, isn't it?' asked Lowe, pouring some brandy out into a glass.

'Yes, it's my room all right,' answered the other, 'but what's that got to do with it?'

'I'll tell you in a moment.'

After great difficulty, Lowe succeeded in getting the girl to swallow about a tablespoonful of brandy. When he had done this he set the glass down and turned his attention to the unhappy Mr. Willings.

'Now,' he said, 'you say you don't know how this lady came to be in your room? You were either lying when you said you hadn't left your room previously, or you're responsible for the condition of this girl.'

' 'Ow do you make that out?'

There was a silence, and Mr. Willings licked his dry lips. 'Oh, well,' he said, 'I suppose I'd better make a clean breast of it. As a matter of fact I wasn't in this 'ere room all the time. You see, it was like this. I went to bed and went to sleep, but the noise the wind was making and the banging and the creaking woke me up. Lyin' awake I began to feel thirsty, an' I thought 'ow good a nice drop of beer would taste, so I hopped up and pulled on me coat and went down to the bar. I was afraid it might be locked; but the door was open and I went in and drew meself a pint. That's the truth, and there ain't nothin' criminal in that!'

'What time was it when you went down for the beer?' said Lowe.

'I couldn't tell you that,' answered the other. 'But it wasn't very long before your friend came round waking everybody up.'

'When you went down for the beer,' said Lowe, 'did you see or hear anybody about?'

The little man hesitated before replying.

'Well I did and I didn't,' he said at length. 'What I mean is, I thought there was somebody about, but I may 'ave been mistaken. The wind was making funny noises.'

'You heard something,' said Trevor Lowe quickly, and again there was a hesitation before he got a reply.

23

'Well, yes, I did,' said Mr. Willings reluctantly. 'And it wasn't so much what I 'eard as what I felt. I could 'ave sworn that while I was drawin' that there beer I was bein' watched.'

'Did you see someone then?' asked Shadgold, as he paused.

The little man shook his head.

'No, I didn't see no one, and I didn't properly 'ear anyone. It was just a feelin'.'

'H'm!' said Lowe. 'Well, you ought to have told us all this before. After you'd had your beer and got back to your room, did you hear anything then?'

'No, nothing,' was the answer. 'I was so perishin' cold that I pulled the bedclothes right up over me head and tried to get warm again.'

Before Lowe could frame the next question, a long quivering sigh from the girl attracted his attention; and, bending over the bed, he saw that her eyes were open. She was gazing up at him blankly without any sign of recognition, and as he stooped closer he saw that her lips were moving. No words came at first, and then faintly — so faintly as to be almost inaudible — she spoke.

'The Christmas card,' she whispered. 'Don't let them get it. Don't let — '

The feeble voice faded away into silence. Her eyes closed, and with another long sigh she relapsed into unconsciousness again.

There came a hurried step outside the door of the little parlour and a second later it was thrown open. Shadgold, breathing a little quickly and with his red face flushed with excitement, came in hastily.

'I've made a discovery, Lowe,' he jerked. 'I've found out what Makepiece was.'

Lowe looked up interestedly. He had been sitting thoughtfully in front of the fire.

'What was he?' he asked.

'You heard of Cranston and Small?' said the inspector, and a curious light came into Trevor Lowe's eyes as he nodded.

'You mean the firm of private investigators who handle so much divorce work?' he said.

'They're the people,' answered Shadgold. 'Well, William Makepiece was on their staff. He was a detective!'

There was no doubt about the dead

25

man's identity; the contents of a wallet which Shadgold had found in his room provided ample testimony in the shape of letters and several visiting cards.

'A detective, was he?' said Lowe thoughtfully. 'H'm. Well, that gives us a new angle. His firm will be able to state what business he was engaged on, and that may help.'

'If he was engaged on any,' answered the inspector. 'You've always got to take into consideration, Mr. Lowe, that this is the holiday season. He may only have been on his way to spend Christmas somewhere.'

'The thing that puzzles me, Shadgold, is the torn half of that Christmas card. Where is the other half? Did the person who killed Makepiece remove it; and if so, why didn't he remove the whole? There was obviously no struggle, so it didn't get torn accidentally. And what has the girl got to do with it?'

There came a tap on the door, and without waiting for an invitation the surly-faced landlord slouched in, a worried look on his unpleasant face. He stopped just within the open doorway and looked from one to the other hesitantly.

'What is it? What do you want?' growled Shadgold.

Cornford advanced another step and cleared his throat. When he spoke his voice was dry and husky.

'I wanted to have a word with yer,' he said.

'Do you know something?' snapped the Scotland Yard man eagerly.

The landlord nodded slowly.

'Yes, I know somethin',' he replied. 'Tain't much, but I think I oughta tell yer.' He seemed to find some difficulty in putting his story into words, and they waited expectantly and impatiently. 'It's like this,' said Cornford, after a pause. 'One of those fellers 'as been lying to yer. I can prove — '

What he could prove they never knew, for at that instant from outside the room came a sharp, spitting crack, and the landlord's face sagged. His jaw dropped and his little black eyes opened wide. A stupid look of astonishment crossed his ugly face, and both his hands went to his back. He tried to speak, groaned, and fell forward.

With a startled exclamation Lowe caught him as he slumped to the ground, easing his fall.

A second shot whistled past Shadgold's ear as he made a dash for the door, and then a heavy object struck him in the face; with a cry of pain he staggered backwards. There was a sharp thud as something fell on the floor of the little room.

The man in Lowe's arms gave a convulsive shudder and his head fell limply backwards. Lowe took one look at the landlord's face and knew that Joe Cornford would never utter the words he had been about to speak. He was dead! And the weapon that had killed him lay a few feet away, shining dully blue in the light from the lamp on the table.

5

As he lowered the limp form of the landlord to the floor, Trevor Lowe heard an excited shout followed by the sound of running feet; a second later Arnold White appeared in the open doorway.

'What was the shooting?' he began, and stopped abruptly as he saw the thing at the dramatist's feet.

'That's what the shooting was,' said Lowe grimly, pointing down at all that was left of Joe Cornford. 'He was shot through the doorway. Did you see anyone?'

White shook his head.

'Not a soul,' he replied. 'I was upstairs having a wash when I heard the shots, and hurried down at once, but I saw no one.'

Shadgold, dabbing at the red weal across his face, grunted savagely.

'I'm going to find out where everyone was,' he growled, and without waiting for a reply he strode across the hall to the coffee-room. Jerking open the door, he glared in.

The meek-faced Mr. Pilbeam was sitting hunched up in a chair before the fire. He was apparently asleep, for he jumped up with a start when Shadgold spoke.

'Where are the others?' demanded the Scotland Yard man, glaring round the empty room.

'I — I don't know,' stammered Mr. Pilbeam. 'They were here when I fell asleep.'

The burly inspector eyed him suspiciously.

'Been asleep, have you?' he snapped. 'You sure of that?'

'C-c-course I'm sure,' stammered the meek little man. 'Y-y-you woke me up, bursting in like that.'

'H'm! Well, you stay where you are.' The inspector swung round as a murmur of startled voices reached his ears. The rest of the party were crowding down the staircase, and bringing up the rear was the unkempt figure of Mrs. Cornford, the landlady.

'What was all that bangin'?' demanded Arty Willings, as he saw Shadgold. 'Sounded like somebody shootin'.'

'It was somebody shooting,' answered the Scotland Yard man curtly. 'Where have you people been?'

A chorus of voices answered him. They had all been up to their rooms to dress. It seemed useless to expect to get any more sleep that night and, scantily clad as they were, they had begun to feel chilly in spite of the fire in the coffee-room, so they had decided to slip up to their rooms and dress.

'Well, you can all go into the coffee-room,' snapped Shadgold, 'and you can stay there, do you understand? No one is to leave that room without my permission.'

At that moment the voice of the landlady came to him, and Lowe went out into the hall to see what she wanted. He found her standing on the stairs.

'You asked me to tell yer,' said the woman, 'when that girl was awake. Well, she is.'

'Good!' said the dramatist. 'I'll come up at once.'

The woman led the way to the room and stood aside for him to enter.

The girl's big grey eyes were open, and looked large and almost black in the dead whiteness of her face. Trevor Lowe went over to the bed and sat on the edge.

'Feeling better, Miss Lake?' he asked kindly.

She nodded slowly.

'Yes, thank you,' she answered. 'What

— what happened?'

Lowe told her how they had found her. She gave a little shiver.

'I don't remember anything,' she said. 'I went to bed and fell asleep almost at once. Soon afterwards I was dimly conscious of someone standing over me, then something very painful struck me on the head. After that I remember nothing until I woke up and found myself here.'

'Have you any idea, Miss Lake, why this attack should have been made on you?'

She hesitated, her big eyes searching his face, and then she nodded again.

'Yes, I think I do,' she answered faintly. 'I'm sure I do.'

Trevor Lowe leaned forward.

'Then will you tell me, Miss Lake?' he said. 'I assure you it's not with any wish to pry into your affairs that I ask; but a serious crime was committed here last night, apart from the attack on you, and another one has just taken place.'

'Crime?' she said, and her eyes grew dark with fear.

'Yes, murder,' he replied gravely.

She drew in her breath with a quick little hiss.

'Who — who was killed?' she asked.

'That stout, jolly-faced man,' said Lowe, watching her keenly. 'William Makepiece.'

The name apparently conveyed nothing to her, for the expression on her face did not change.

'How — how dreadful!' she whispered. And then: 'Who are you?'

'My name is Trevor Lowe,' answered the dramatist.

The fear died from her eyes and a look of relief came into her pale face.

'I've heard of you,' she said.

'Who were you frightened of?' he asked. She shook her head.

'I don't know,' she replied. 'That's the dreadful part of it!'

'I think you had better tell me everything,' he said, as she paused.

'I will,' she answered. 'But it's rather a difficult story — I mean, it's not very easy to tell to a stranger — and I don't quite know where to begin.'

'Tell me why you were attacked,' said Lowe. 'Do you know why?'

'Oh yes,' she answered at once. 'I was attacked because of something I possess!' She smiled rather sadly, and added hastily: 'I haven't any money. I've so little that I don't know how I've managed to live during the last year, but I've got something that's worth roughly about half a million pounds!'

Lowe stared at her in amazement.

'You've got something that's worth half a million pounds?' he echoed incredulously. 'Do you mean you've got it here?'

She nodded, and a little glimmer of amusement crept into her eyes at the astonishment that her words had created.

'Yes, I've got it here,' she said. 'At least, I've got half of it. What I have isn't worth a cent all by itself. You see, this is the way of it, Mr. Lowe. I'm going to start really from the beginning; I'll make it as brief as I can.' Her voice was stronger now and a tinge of colour had crept into the creamy whiteness of her cheeks. 'I'd better start by telling you,' she went on, 'that my name isn't Lake. Lake is the name I've been known by all my life, but my real name is Lanning.'

Trevor Lowe started.

'You're not any relation to Sir Joshua Lanning?' he asked.

'Yes,' she said. 'I'm his daughter!'

Lowe's brows contracted. The daughter of Sir Joshua Lanning, the steel millionaire!

'Please go on, Miss Lanning,' he said. 'I'm very interested!'

'As I said,' she continued, 'it's very difficult. Although I'm Sir Joshua Lanning's daughter, I've never seen him. You see, my mother divorced him when I was two years old, and she was given the custody of the child. She was very bitter against my father, and she took me away, returning to her maiden name of Lake. My father, I believe, begged and prayed her not to go; but when she insisted, he gave her an envelope, and said that if at any time she wished to return to him and remarry him she had only to send the contents of the envelope and he would come to her, wherever she was.

'My mother told me this just before she died, seven years ago, but she also made me promise that I would never go near my father unless he should first seek me

35

out. I had no money and I had to earn my living, which I succeeded in doing more or less — mostly less. And then a week ago I saw in a newspaper an advertisement. It had been put in by a firm of solicitors, and briefly stated that if Miss Iris Lake, or Lanning, would call on the advertisers she would hear something to her advantage.

'I guessed that it concerned my father, and I went. Mr. Thompson, the head of the firm, told me at once that they had had over a hundred applicants, but that he had soon assured himself that they were none of them the person he was looking for. If I were really that person there would be one means of identification, and only one, which would satisfy him.

'I knew what he meant, of course — the envelope which my father had given my mother. I told the solicitor that I knew what he meant, without exactly telling him what the thing was. He told me that my father was dying and that he was very anxious to find his missing daughter. He had already made a will in her favour.

'He asked me if I would travel down to

Tregoney, where my father was living, taking with me the means of identification which I had mentioned. He wrote to my father saying that I would arrive on the twenty-third, and I was on my way when the snow block forced us to spend the night here.'

'And this means of identification that you were taking with you?' asked Lowe, although he knew before she answered.

'Was the half of a Christmas card,' she replied. 'A Christmas card that my mother had sent to my father the Christmas before they were married. He had torn it in half, keeping one half and putting the other half in the envelope which he gave her.'

'I see,' said Lowe softly. 'And where is your half?'

'Go along to the room I occupied and fetch my shoes,' she said.

When he came back with them she struggled up to a sitting posture and, taking the left one, pulled out the lining of the sole. Between it and the sole itself was an envelope; and, opening this, she drew out the torn half of an old and faded Christmas card.

'That's it,' she said.

Lowe looked at it.

'If that's your half,' he said slowly, 'and the other half is in the possession of your father, then how does the third 'half' come into it?'

She looked at him, puzzled.

'The third half? What do you mean?' she asked.

'I mean,' replied Trevor Lowe, 'that I found half a Christmas card in the hand of the dead man, William Makepiece.'

6

'Well, it's a queer story,' remarked Detective Inspector Shadgold thoughtfully an hour later, when Trevor Lowe had repeated to him what he had learned from Iris Lanning. 'And it's a queer business. I don't quite see how this fellow Makepiece fits in.'

'I should imagine that the solicitors had engaged him, unknown to the girl, to keep an eye on her,' said Lowe.

'You mean they expected something

might happen?' said the Scotland Yard man.

'It's not unnatural, is it?' asked Lowe. 'The torn piece of cardboard she was carrying about with her is worth something in the nature of half a million — a big enough bait for any crook to have a bite at!'

'Still, it wouldn't be any good without the girl,' argued Shadgold.

'Oh, my dear fellow,' protested Lowe, 'think for a moment! The last time Sir Joshua Lanning saw his daughter she was two years old; he hasn't seen her since. Any girl would do, provided she could produce the necessary form of identification.'

'H'm, yes, I suppose you're right,' grunted the Scotland Yard man. 'But the solicitors had seen her.'

'The solicitors had seen a girl who said she was the girl they were advertising for,' answered the dramatist. 'They had no proof that she was, except her word that she had the necessary identification. Until she had shown her half of the Christmas card to Sir Joshua Lanning, nobody could tell whether she was the right girl or not.'

'Then it's your opinion,' said Shadgold, 'that the idea was to secure the girl's half and substitute someone else in her place?'

'Exactly,' replied Lowe, nodding. 'Makepiece had to die because he knew the real Iris Lanning; but if we had found in the morning that the two of them were missing, everyone would have thought that they had gone of their own free will. No doubt the killer would have tidied up the rooms and made it look like that.'

'That's suggesting that he knew who Makepiece was and why he was here,' said Shadgold.

'I'm suggesting just that,' answered Lowe.

'And how do you account for the torn half of the Christmas card found in Makepiece's hand?' demanded the Scotland Yard man.

Trevor Lowe frowned and shook his head.

'I can't account for it,' he replied frankly, 'but there must be some explanation. Let me look at it again.'

Shadgold thrust his hand into his pocket and produced his wallet. From it he extracted the torn Christmas card and handed it to the dramatist.

Trevor Lowe carried it over to the lamp and examined it carefully. It was obviously a new card; the ragged edges were clean and unsoiled. In turning it sideways he noticed something that he had not seen before. In one corner were a number of indentations. A closer inspection revealed the letter D and the figures 2 and 1. Above and below these were indistinguishable marks forming two semicircles.

An idea suddenly occurred to Lowe, and taking out the envelope he had found in the girl's room — and which he had put in his pocket — he compared the postmark with the marks on the card. It had been posted on December the twenty-first. The stamp had been rather heavily impressed and had marked the enclosed card. He showed his discovery to Shadgold.

'There's very little doubt', he said, 'that this card I found in Makepiece's hand originally came out of this envelope. I wonder if it was the girl who tore this card,' he continued slowly, 'and left half

41

in the envelope as a blind to make anyone think it was the important card — the piece that was hidden in her shoe.'

'It sounds possible,' said Shadgold. 'Why not ask her?'

'I will,' said Lowe, 'and test this half Makepiece had with the genuine half.'

He returned in less than a minute.

'That's cleared that up,' he said. 'She tore a Christmas card she had received in half and left one half in the envelope so that anyone finding it would think it was the real card. You know what conclusion this leads to? That it was Makepiece who searched the girl's room. In which case he was responsible for knocking her out, tying her up and putting her in that cupboard. But he wasn't responsible for sticking that knife into his heart. I think the person who did that did the rest.'

'The question is, who?' growled the inspector. He took a glass round behind the bar and, grasping one of the handles, held it under the tap. Nothing happened. With a snort of disgust he tried the other. He tried all three with a like result. 'I suppose there's nothing more to do until the local police arrive?'

'No, I suppose not,' said the dramatist, a little absently, and then: 'What happened to Mrs. Cornford?'

Shadgold looked at him, rather surprised.

'I packed her off to her room,' he answered. 'She wasn't in a fit state to remain up.'

'I'd like to have a word with her,' murmured Lowe. 'Wait here, I shan't be long.'

He left the bar and made his way upstairs. Outside the room in which the girl lay he came upon his secretary, who had been relegated to the job of keeping guard.

'Anybody been near?' he asked, and White shook his head.

'No,' he replied.

Trevor Lowe nodded and passed on. Mrs. Cornford's room was on the first floor above, and reaching it he tapped on the door. At first there was no reply, but at the second knock the old woman's voice called and wanted to know who was there.

'It's Trevor Lowe,' replied the dramatist. 'Can I have a word with you?'

He heard the creak of a bed, the pad of
bare feet crossing the floor, and then the
door was opened an inch.

'What do you want with me?' asked the
woman dully.

'I want to ask you a question,' he replied.

She looked at him curiously when she
heard what he wanted to know.

'Not for nearly a year,' she said.

'You're sure of that?' he asked, and she
nodded.

Shadgold was staring out of the
window at the cold grey of the coming
morning when Lowe came back.

'Well?' he grunted.

'Very well,' answered Lowe cheerfully,
and there was a note of satisfaction in his
voice. 'I think we're nearing the end of
this business.'

The Scotland Yard man stared at him
incredulously.

'If you'll ask Willings to come in for a
moment I'll show you.'

Shadgold hesitated, and then shrugged
his shoulders.

'Oh, well, I suppose you know what you're getting at,' he said, and crossing over to the door went out.

He was gone some little time, and when he returned was accompanied by the sleepy-eyed Arty Willings, who yawned openly as he slouched in.

'I want your help, Mr. Willings,' said the dramatist genially.

The little cockney eyed him suspiciously.

'You said,' explained Lowe, 'that when you came down in the night you had a feeling that you were being watched.'

'That's right,' said Mr. Willings, nodding.

'Now, where did you experience this feeling?' Lowe went on. 'While you were coming down the stairs? While you were in here? Or as you were returning to your room?'

'While I was in here,' answered the other, after a momentary hesitation.

'But you neither heard anything nor saw anyone?' said Lowe, and Mr. Willings shook his head.

'No, I told you that before,' he replied. 'It was only a feelin' I 'ad.'

'Was the coffee-room door closed?'

45

'Yes,' answered Mr. Willings after a little thought.

'I see,' murmured the dramatist. 'Now, would you mind showing us exactly what you did when you came down?'

'I came in 'ere,' said the little cockney, 'went over to the bar, and had a glass of beer.'

'Show us what you did,' repeated Lowe, and Mr. Willings obeyed.

He went round behind the long counter, picked up a glass, and stretched out his hand to the centre of the three beer handles.

'Just a minute,' interrupted Lowe. 'You poured yourself out a glass of draught beer? You didn't open a bottle or draw it from the cask?'

'No,' said Arty Willings. 'I prefer draught beer. And mighty good it was!'

'And then you returned to your room and went to bed?' said the dramatist.

'That's right,' answered Mr. Willings.

'H'm!' said Lowe. 'And during this time the murderer was secreting Miss Lake in the cupboard in your room. Let's see if we can imagine what he did. He left his room when he thought the whole house was quiet and sleeping and made his way along to the girl's. He knew that she had in her possession an object that was worth a considerable amount of money. He rendered her unconscious with a blow from some instrument like a sandbag. He was disturbed for a moment, and dodged out on the roof with the senseless girl. Afterwards he climbed back and carried the girl, whom he had bound and gagged, along to your room and locked her in the cupboard.

'He then went back to search her belongings for the thing he wanted, and he found it — or thought he had found it — in her handbag. He was afraid to stop in her room and examine it closely, for there was no means of locking the door, and there was a chance that he might be surprised by one of the other inhabitants of the inn. He brought it down to the coffee-room, lit the lamp and found to his dismay that he had been tricked. The thing he had taken so much trouble to get was a fake.

'He had just decided to make another search of the girl's room when William

Makepiece appeared in the doorway, and demanded that he hand over the object he had taken and which was still in his hand.

'Makepiece informed him that he was a detective who had been employed to see that no harm came to the girl. The man, whom we will call X for the moment, saw his whole plan being ruined by this unexpected intruder. No doubt Makepiece threatened him; probably there was a brief struggle for possession of the precious object that X had taken such pains to secure. The safest way to stop Makepiece from keeping it, and also from babbling afterwards, was to kill him. This X did, and so became a murderer.

'He placed the worthless article in Makepiece's hand, to leave a false clue to suggest that it was Makepiece who had ransacked the girl's case.

'He was clever,' continued Lowe, 'but like so many crooks, he wasn't clever enough. He made a mistake. If you fetch me the thing he took from the girl's room I'll show you what that mistake was, Willings.'

Lowe nodded casually towards the far corner of the bar on which lay several objects, among them the torn card which he had taken from Makepiece's hand. Mr. Willings went over, picked it up, and handed it to the detective.

'Thank you,' said Lowe, and his eyes gleamed. 'I said just now that the murderer made a mistake. As a matter of fact he made two. He's just made the second — a mistake I was hoping he would make. I never mentioned what the object was that he took from Miss Lake's room. Nobody knew, except Inspector Shadgold, my secretary, and myself, that the torn half of a Christmas card was found in the dead man's hand. How did you know, Willings?'

The colour fled from the little cockney's face, leaving it a dirty white

'I don't know,' he began. 'I — '

'You knew,' snapped Lowe sternly, 'because it was you who took this card out of Miss Lake's handbag in the first place. You who tied her up and locked her in your cupboard. You who came downstairs and later killed William Makepiece.

You who, when the girl was found, lied and said that you had felt thirsty and came down to this bar and drawn yourself beer.'

'You're talking nonsense!' cried the man. 'You're trying to frame this on me! I did come down to get a drink! All I've told you is true!' In his excitement all trace of his cockney accent had vanished, and Lowe was quick to remark on it.

'You've forgotten your accent, Mr. Willings,' he said softly. 'The same as you forgot to verify your facts concerning your story of the beer.'

'What do you mean?' muttered the other.

'I mean,' retorted Trevor Lowe curtly, 'that that beer engine has not been connected for a year! That's what Cornford was going to tell us when you shot him. It was absolutely impossible for you to have drawn any beer that way. That, coupled with the fact that you fell into the trap I had prepared for you, has given you away. No one but the man who searched Miss Lake's room could have known what the object was I referred to, and yet you went and fetched it without my telling you — fetched it from among half a dozen other objects, all of which might equally have been the right one.'

The trapped man's lips drew back from his teeth in a snarl. Without warning he picked up a wooden stool that stood in front of the bar and hurled it at Trevor Lowe's head.

'I suppose you think you've got me?' he cried harshly. 'But you haven't, yet!'

Lowe dodged the stool and it went crashing through the window, ripping out glass and woodwork — and then Shadgold took a hand. As Willings made a dash for the door, he barred his path and gripped him by the arm.

'No you don't!' he growled; and the revolver with which Willings had shot the landlord appeared in his other hand. 'You just keep quiet. If you can find any rope, Lowe, we'll tie him up until the police arrive.'

* * *

The police patrol was stopped as he passed the inn and given the news and instructions. Later came a sleepy-eyed inspector and a constable. They came in a car, and when they went away they were accompanied by the man who called himself Arty Willings.

Later on that morning, when the snow had stopped falling and a pale sun shone coldly on the expanse of white, a car which Lowe had asked the police to send from Bugle arrived and drove the dramatist, Shadgold, Arnold White and the girl to Tregoney, where they left her to meet the father she had never seen.

It was on the morning of Christmas day that Trevor Lowe heard the last echo of that sinister business at the gloomy inn. Shadgold had just returned from Bugle and an interview with the police. Arty Willings had been identified as Montague Buxton, a cousin of Sir Joshua Lanning, and when he found that the game was up he made a full confession. It tallied almost exactly with Lowe's theory.

The old man had told Buxton the story of his efforts to find his missing daughter, and gradually the idea had taken shape in Buxton's brain to put forward a substitute.

He had led a fairly wild life and was associated with a woman who had few scruples that money could not overrule. He had confided his plans to her, and she had agreed to present herself to Sir Joshua as his missing relative. Buxton, who had been staying with the old man, was aware that he was prepared to accept anyone who could produce the torn half of the Christmas card which matched his own.

In order to keep an eye on the girl he had disguised himself as the rather insignificant-looking cockney, and had met the Western Express from Paddington at Bodmin. The original idea was to kidnap the girl at Tregoney; but when they had all been forced to spend the night at the Chained Man, this had been altered.

'There's plenty of evidence against him,' the Scotland Yard man concluded. 'I should think the jury would bring in a verdict without leaving the box.'

'Well, he deserves what he gets,' said Trevor Lowe, 'if ever a man did.'

The Mystery of the Unfortunate Undertaker

as related by Nelson Jarvis, F.R.I.B.A.,
to Gerald Verner

Note by Mr. Nelson Jarvis: When it was first suggested to me that I should relate some of those cases of Mr. Lattimer Shrive's with which I am intimately associated, I approached the great private detective rather diffidently, knowing his dislike of anything in the nature of publicity. 'By all means, Jarvis,' he said. 'I hope, however, that you will curb your somewhat juvenile love of the purely sensational, and select those problems which appeal more to the intellect than to the emotions.' I have endeavoured to carry out his wishes in this respect. Of the cases which I have chosen for publication, some are strange, some terrible, and some merely fantastic; but none, I think, is unleavened by that appeal to the intellect to which my friend Shrive referred.

One bizarre case with which my friend Mr. Lattimer Shrive was connected began, I recollect, on an unpleasant day in early December: cold and raw, with the promise of a thick fog later.

I had been feeling strangely depressed all the morning, and my melancholy was in no wise lessened by the behaviour of my partner, whose ebullience seems always to increase as my spirits diminish; good fellow that he is, he tends to fray my nerves by acting as if he invented architecture. And his eagerness to meddle with my work, and his insistence on his own up-to-date knowledge, make me believe that he thinks me something of an old fossil.

At any rate, soon after luncheon I told him that I thought I would leave for the day. I had decided to call on Lattimer Shrive, whom I had not seen for several weeks, for a smoke and a chat to cheer me up.

A taxi took me to Piccadilly and into

the courtyard of that building on the north side known as Albany, where Shrive has lived for many years. 'I knew this place, Jarvis,' he sometimes says, 'when the great ones of the earth lived here. Byron, for instance. I well remember drinking gin and water with Byron on one occasion in his chambers here. Of course, I was not much more than a boy at the time, you understand . . . ' And his dark, deep-set eyes twinkle at me mischievously. I well understand what he means. He is referring to an occasion when, being for professional purposes in the disguise of an old, old man, he convinced some antique dame at a Belgrave Square tea party that he had met the author of *Don Juan*. You may doubt whether a man in the prime of life could pass, however skilfully disguised, for a centenarian. If you do doubt it, I can only assure you that the stage would have gained a very great actor and prince of pretence if Lattimer Shrive had ever trod the boards.

Well, up the stone steps of Albany I went, receiving a salute from the top-hatted porter, and made my way along the glass-topped avenue, known as the Rope-Walk, which is flanked by chambers on either side. As I turned into Shrive's block I felt, suddenly, a lightening of the heart. It always does me good to see my old friend.

He opened the door of his chambers himself in answer to my ring, and his saturnine face lit up with pleasure as he saw me standing there. He was clad in his familiar butcher-blue workman's smock, which he had bought in France many years before, and a pair of ancient sponge bag trousers.

'My dear fellow, come in,' he said, ushering me into the huge, untidy room that served him as study and office. 'Pull up a chair to the fire — nothing like a coal fire, is there? — and make yourself comfortable. I'll ring for Mrs. Bedlow to bring tea.' His keen eyes scrutinised me. 'Dear me, I'm sorry to see that your secretary is ill. Nothing serious, I hope?'

'She is away with a cold,' I answered. 'But how, may I ask, did you know that?'

He chuckled softly.

'It's always a pleasure to exercise any

57

slight talent one may possess on you, Jarvis,' he said. 'But it's really so simple that I hardly like to explain. You have told me that your secretary is in the habit of brushing your coat and hat each day when you leave the office. Both your coat and hat have, however, quite obviously not received this attention for several days. Your secretary has been with you for a great many years and it is unlikely that she would have suddenly left you. She has, to my knowledge, no relations for whom she would absent herself from business for any period worth mentioning. Ergo — she must be ill.'

'It's simple enough when you explain it,' I grunted, filling my pipe from his tobacco jar: and a wonderful tobacco it was, blended by Shrive personally. If my friend were interested in making money, he could realise a fortune by putting it on the market. As it is, he makes up enough for himself and an occasional two-pound tin for a friend. Mr. James Agate is among these; and in one of his *Ego* volumes, unless I am much mistaken, there is a dithyramb called 'The Best Christmas

Present of my Life' on it.

'Here's something that may prove more difficult,' Shrive said, rummaging among the papers on his littered writing-table. 'See what you make of that, Jarvis.'

He tossed over a letter. It bore a printed heading: *J. Drapkin, Undertaker and Funeral Furnisher, 1993b, Clapham Rise, S.W.*, and it was dated the previous day.

Dear Sir (it ran in a rather crabbed hand)

I am taking the liberty of writing to you in the hope that you can help me. May I call on you tomorrow afternoon at 4.30? I am at my wits' end, and the matter has become serious. Do please see me — I beg you in the name of heaven to see me.

Your obedient servant,
Joseph Drapkin.

'He seems to be in a mighty stew about something,' I commented as I handed back the letter.

Shrive looked grave.

'Yes,' he agreed, 'There is more than a suspicion of panic in that final appeal . . . ' He hesitated as the doorbell rang: a jerky, uncertain ring, as though pressed by a nervous and agitated finger. 'That should be our friend Drapkin,' he said. 'It is just after half-past four.'

'You would like me to go?' I suggested.

'By no means, my dear fellow. The interview promises to be of interest, and I should welcome your opinion. We will, if you have no objection, postpone our tea until afterwards . . . '

Mrs. Bedlow, Shrive's elderly Irish housekeeper, announced the visitor in her usual manner, which was funereal to say the least: as Shrive sometimes remarked, not even Mrs. Siddons herself had a more striking charnel-house voice. He was a small man, so excessively thin that he seemed to have no flesh on his bones at all. His tiny boot-button eyes looked out from deep hollows, and his pallor was pitiful.

Shrive welcomed him with the distinguished courtesy which was one of his characteristics, introduced me, and sat him down in an armchair facing the window.

'It's very good of you to see me, sir,' said the undertaker gratefully. 'I shall be pleased to pay you any fee . . . '

'We'll discuss that when you have told me how I can be of service,' interrupted Shrive. 'Doubtless you will have something to tell me about your contemplated trip abroad.'

'Abroad?' repeated the little man, looking whiter than ever about the gills. 'How did you . . . ?'

'Well,' smiled Shrive, 'if you will go about with an overseas airways brochure sticking out of the side pocket of your overcoat . . . But never mind that, my dear sir.'

The undertaker burst into excited speech. 'I was thinking of going abroad, sir. I was. And I'll tell you why, sir. To get away from it all. To cease being the victim of malicious and devilish persecution. And it's well-nigh driving me insane, sir!'

Shrive and I exchanged the briefest glance, for the illusion of persecution is a fairly common mental disorder.

'What form,' asked my friend, 'does this persecution take? And who is it that is persecuting you?'

'It's taken several forms,' answered Drapkin. 'For instance, a couple of weeks ago thirty or forty full-grown rats were introduced in some way into my establishment . . . '

'Rats?'

'Yes, Mr. Shrive. Filthy brown brutes! It was a terrible job getting rid of them. And they're not all gone yet . . . ' His voice rose rather hysterically.

'*Rattus norvegicus*,' mused Shrive, 'which reached England from Russia in 1728, was not an immigrant that gives us any cause to be grateful. I remember old Professor Blackie telling me that once, when he was experimenting on the brown rat, or Hanoverian rat as it used to be called, he . . . But enough of that! Will you continue, Mr. Drapkin?' I knew Shrive well enough to be certain that this digression had been calculated. He was giving the undertaker an opportunity to take a grip on himself.

'A few days later,' the visitor went on

more calmly, 'I woke up one morning to find a most unpleasant smell everywhere about the place. Like rotten eggs, only worse, much worse. It was really dreadful, sir. I thought it must be the drains until I discovered that somebody had saturated the place during the night with some foul-smelling chemical . . . '

'I gather,' interposed Shrive, 'that you live over your business premises?'

'Yes, sir.'

'Alone?'

'Yes, I am a widower. As a matter of fact, sir, my dear wife died three years ago yesterday. But until two months ago I had an assistant who lived in.'

'Has he left you since?'

'Well, you see, sir, he was run over and killed by a lorry.'

'Dear me,' said Shrive. 'Dear me.'

'The next thing that happened — not to put too fine a point on it — was more serious. If you'll believe me, sir, someone tampered with my morning milk . . . '

'Poisoned it?'

'I don't know, sir. But I always give the cat a saucerful first thing, and it made

63

him as sick as — well, as a cat. I naturally didn't touch it after that.'

Shrive stared inscrutably at the ceiling. 'Has there been any other form of persecution?'

'Yes, Mr. Shrive. It was what prompted me to write to you.' The undertaker leaned forward impressively. 'Not to put too fine a point on it, I think somebody is trying to murder me. Three nights ago a personal attack was made on me. I had been out late on business and was returning home, by way of a quiet street, when a car drew up at the kerb beside me. A man jumped out and attempted to throw a blanket over my head. Some people came to my assistance, and the car drove off.'

'You would recognise that man again?'

Drapkin shook his head. 'No, it was a dark night,' he said.

'You know of no one who bears you a grudge?'

'No one.'

'Have you been to the police?'

'Well, sir . . . yes, sir. Not to put too fine a point on it, Mr. Shrive, they don't seem to believe me. They think I'm — well — *batty*, if you know the word.'

'I know it,' said Shrive calmly. 'It derives, you understand, from the term 'bats in the belfry'.' He stared at the ceiling again.

There was a long pause. 'What do you advise me to do, Mr. Shrive?' asked the undertaker at last, with an uneasy glance from me to the private detective.

'I advise you to go home,' said Lattimer Shrive, 'and remain indoors. See that all your windows are fastened, and bolt your doors. I shall look into the matter and communicate with you tomorrow.'

'You think — not to put too fine a point on it — that I am in danger?'

'Not if you do as I suggest. By the way, what was the name of your assistant?'

'Letts — Richard Letts.'

'Thank you. I shall be communicating with you, Mr. Drapkin, some time during tomorrow afternoon . . . '

When our visitor had gone, Lattimer Shrive looked at me with a slight twinkle in that eye of his which so much resembled Mr. Gladstone's. 'Well, what do you make of it, Jarvis?' he inquired.

I confessed that I could make nothing of it.

'Think it over,' he said. 'Not to put too fine a point on it,' — and his eye twinkled again — 'you will probably come to the same conclusion as I have. I think perhaps it was a very fortunate thing for our unfortunate friend that he came to me when he did. Otherwise . . . '

'What do you think would have happened?' I asked as he paused. 'Murder?'

'Possibly — possibly not. No, on the whole I think not.'

Then, leaping to his feet, he broke out: '*Toast*, my dear fellow — hot buttered toast. I will not be kept from it any longer. And a cup of tea so strong that it would make a cat speak.' He pressed the bell.

* * *

There was a telephone message from Shrive waiting for me when I got back from luncheon on the following day. It merely asked me to meet him at ten o'clock that night at 1993b Clapham Rise.

And the night was even worse than the previous one had been. The taxi moved at a snail's pace through the yellow-ochre fog, and the street lamps swam powerlessly in the murk. When I eventually did arrive, half an hour late, the undertaker's establishment was in complete darkness. I tapped uncertainly on the side door. It was opened instantly, and Lattimer Shrive's voice whispered out of the blackness: 'Come in, Jarvis.' He grabbed me by the arm and guided me up the stairs.

'I'm afraid you'll have to put up with the darkness,' he said. 'We dare not risk a light. You know Inspector Martin, of course.'

I could just distinguish the bulky form of the Inspector as I wished him good evening, and that was all.

'Where is Drapkin?' I asked in a whisper.

'He departed for the country, with great ostentation, early this afternoon,' said Shrive with a chuckle. 'We have put a notice in the window to the effect that owing to family bereavement the place will be closed until next week.'

Inspector Martin gave a grim, short laugh. 'What they call an undertaker's holiday!'

'For what reason has he gone?' I inquired.

'That,' Shrive replied, 'I hope you will see before the night is over. And now I think it better that we refrain from talking. Sound carries in this foggy quietness.'

Then began our vigil in the front room. Not unnaturally I was bewildered, and consumed with curiosity to know why we were there at all. The time passed slowly — oh, so slowly. I heard a church clock strike eleven; and three or four hours later it managed to strike half-past eleven. The place was very still except for an occasional faint sound from the street outside. And just after twelve there was another sound that did *not* come from without. It was a faint splintering crack, and it came from below.

'He's here,' whispered Lattimer Shrive, his lips close to my ear. 'Come along, but don't make a sound . . . '

We tiptoed out of the room to the head of the stair. Below, out through the arch that led to the shop, a faint spark of light glinted and went out. Moving like cats, we crept down the stairs until we could see into the dark, shuttered shop. A figure was fanning the light from a dimmed torch among the coffins on their trestles. Then there was a sudden 'click' and the place became flooded with light

'I'm afraid,' said Lattimer Shrive sternly, his hand still on the switch, 'that you are wasting your time, Mr. Edwards. You see, we found the Stirling Emeralds, where your friend Letts hid them, earlier this afternoon . . . '

The man said not a word but flung himself in the direction of Shrive, who executed an evasive movement worthy of a ballet dancer. It was Inspector Martin who took the shock; and the criminal, the coffins and the law were all piled on the floor together.

Shrive looked at me and chuckled. 'Brawn, my dear fellow, is useful sometimes, and Martin has plenty of that. Whereas I, of course, have the brains . . . '

* * *

'It was really a very simple case,' remarked Lattimer Shrive some two hours later, as we sat before a blazing fire in his Albany chambers. 'It was quite evident that the various forms of persecution — the rats, the unpleasant chemical, the doctored milk, and, finally, the attempted abduction — levelled against our unfortunate friend were planned with one object — to force him out of his house for a spell. And if this was the object then there must be something in the house that somebody wanted. It was also obvious that if this person knew exactly where this object was he could have broken in while Drapkin was out, and secured it. But he wanted more time to search for it, so it must have been hidden in some place of which he had no knowledge. Now who could have hidden it? Drapkin lived alone, but he had had at one time an assistant who lived on the premises, and this assistant had been run over and killed instantly. If *he* had hidden this thing, whatever it was, he was no

70

longer in a position to reveal the place. You will agree with me, I hope, that this seemed a plausible working theory?

'Well, I made inquiries concerning this man Letts and learned that he was suspected of associating with one 'Tiny' Edwards, an expert burglar who the police were convinced had been responsible for the theft of the Stirling Emeralds — though, of course, they had no actual evidence against him. This Edwards had made no effort to dispose of the emeralds, and had gone down into Devonshire, presumably to lie low for a while. And naturally he made no attempt to communicate with his accomplice Letts. Imagine his feelings when, on returning to London three weeks ago, he found that Letts had been killed!

'And all the rest, my dear fellow, was plain sailing. I concluded that as soon as the coast was clear he would make an attempt to find the emeralds; and so I gave him the opportunity by sending Drapkin off in a cab filled with luggage, and putting a notice in the window of the shop. You saw the result tonight.'

'Excellent!' I said. 'And where did you find the emeralds?'

'Under a loose board in the floor of the workshop,' replied Lattimer Shrive. He jumped up, went to the door, and peered down the passage. 'I see a light in the kitchen,' he said, 'which means that Mrs. Bedlow is still up. You can take my word for it, my dear fellow, that she will be hurt — positively hurt — if we do not have some hot buttered toast and a cup of strong tea.'

He yawned as he pressed the bell. 'And then, Jarvis, as it's so late, you had better take the spare bedroom, don't you think? Unless, of course, you would like a nice healthy walk in the fog . . . '

The Strange Affair
of the Dancing Parson

as related by Nelson Jarvis, F.RI.B.A.,
to Gerald Verner

In looking through my diary I find that it
was on a Saturday — to be precise, the
ninth of April — that I first became involved
in the mysterious affair of the Reverend
Oswald Willingham and the extraordinary
behaviour of the fair-haired curate.

It was a particularly unpleasant morning for the time of year, cold and wet;
and, since I do not put in an appearance
at the office on Saturdays, I was indulging
in an extra hour in bed, when the
insistent ringing of the telephone bell
awoke me from a very pleasant dream.
In some annoyance I sleepily put the
instrument to my ear and discovered that
the early caller was my friend, Lattimer
Shrive.

'Good morning, Jarvis,' he said. 'I gather from your rather incoherent mumble that I have disturbed you in the midst of your slothful habits. How would you like a weekend in the country?'

I answered, still I'm afraid a little huskily, that I should enjoy it very much.

'Excellent, my dear fellow,' said Shrive. 'Meet me at Waterloo, near the main bookstall, in an hour.'

'Where are we going?' I asked.

'To Dean's Prior,' he replied. 'I am looking into a small matter for the Reverend Oswald Willingham, the vicar of that delightful parish, which promises, I think, to be of unusual interest. I will give you the details during the journey down.'

He rang off and I looked at the clock on my bedside table. It was barely seven. Time means nothing to Shrive. I have known him go to bed when everybody else was thinking of getting up, and get up when other people are contemplating going to bed. Supper and breakfast are interchangeable meals with him — a very disconcerting habit for Mrs. Bedlow, his Irish housekeeper.

I was lucky enough to step out of my front door and straight into a taxi, reaching Waterloo with several minutes to spare. The tall, lean figure of Lattimer Shrive was easily distinguishable. He was wearing the rather striking overcoat of tartan plaid which the Laird of Macbeth had presented to him as a souvenir of his services in solving the mystery of Banquo's ghost, which persisted in haunting the ancestral castle — a very strange affair, the true facts of which I may be permitted to divulge at some future date.

He greeted me with a genial smile.

'Punctual as usual, Jarvis,' he said. 'I see that you were fortunate enough to get a taxi all the way.'

'I was,' I admitted. 'But, my dear Shrive, how do you know?'

'Observation, my dear fellow, observation,' he answered, his deep-set eyes twinkling with that boyish mischief which was part of his charm. 'It is an extremely wet morning, yet your shoes are so glossy that they are almost mirror-like. Quite obviously you have not walked even a short distance. But the bus route and the tube station are quite a long way from your house. *Ergo* — you took a taxi. Our train leaves in four minutes. I think we had better hurry.'

We secured a first-class compartment to ourselves and settled down in opposite corners. When the train drew out, Shrive filled his pipe with his own special blend of tobacco and offered me his pouch.

'No, thank you,' I said. 'I prefer not to smoke on an empty stomach and I had no time for any breakfast.'

'I'm afraid, Jarvis,' he said, 'that I have considerably upset your normal routine. However, I feel sure that you will not regret it. This is a very strange and interesting little problem.'

'I am all eagerness to hear about it,' I replied.

He leaned back in his seat, tobacco smoke wreathing round his head, and half closed his eyes.

'The facts are these,' he began, after a slight pause. 'I shall be interested to hear what you make of them, my dear fellow. About three months ago the Reverend Oswald Willingham, a really delightful

76

country clergyman of the old school, engaged a new curate. This young man, the Reverend Timothy Bimbury, was very highly recommended, and proved to be most satisfactory in every way. He was a hard worker, popular in the parish, and of a very quiet and studious disposition. The Reverend Oswald was delighted with this fresh acquisition — until the Tuesday of last week.'

'What happened then?' I asked, as he paused.

'A most extraordinary thing, Jarvis,' answered Shrive, leaning forward. 'The Reverend Oswald Willingham awoke at about one o'clock in the morning without any very clear idea of what had awakened him. The moonlight was streaming in through his window and, thinking this might have been the cause, he got up to draw the curtains. He had omitted to do this before going to bed because the night had then been very dark and cloudy. The window of his bedroom overlooks a large lawn at the back of the vicarage and, on glancing out, he was surprised to see that his new curate, the Reverend Timothy

Bimbury, was dancing wildly on the grass.'

'Dancing?' I exclaimed in astonishment. Shrive nodded.

'Dancing,' he repeated, 'and clad only in his pyjamas. I imagine it was a really remarkable sight. According to the Reverend Oswald, the curate was executing a kind of ballet dance, leaping high into the air at the end of a series of short runs, and wildly flinging his arms about. Willingham watched for a second or two in shocked amazement and then, pulling on his dressing gown, he went down to demand an explanation for Bimbury's extraordinary conduct.'

'What explanation did the curate offer?' I inquired with interest.

'None,' answered Shrive, looking at me queerly. 'He wasn't there.'

'You don't mean . . . ?' I began.

'I mean,' broke in Lattimer Shrive, emphasising each word with the mouthpiece of his pipe, 'that he had disappeared — completely and utterly — and he hasn't been seen since.'

★   ★   ★

The vicarage at Dean's Prior was a fine old house dating back to the fifteenth century, and the Reverend Oswald Willingham was an equally fine old man, though not dating back quite so far.

We were received with an old-fashioned hospitality that is, alas, becoming very rare; and after an excellent luncheon we retired to our host's study, where Shrive, at his own request, was supplied with a pot of very hot and very strong tea — a horrible brew which he drinks at all hours of the day and night — while we contented ourselves with the more conventional coffee.

Ever since I had heard about the extraordinary behaviour of the Reverend Timothy Bimbury I had been trying to find a solution — but with, I fear, poor results. The only reasonable explanation I could think of was that the poor fellow had suddenly taken leave of his senses.

'But that would not account for his complete and inexplicable disappearance,' said Lattimer Shrive, when I put forward this suggestion. 'Remember, he was wearing nothing but his pyjamas. He could not have gone far in that condition without attracting attention.' He looked across at the worried Mr. Willingham. 'You informed the police, of course?'

'Yes — yes, at once,' answered the vicar. 'They have been able to discover nothing — nothing at all.' He shook his white head.

'H'm . . . Ah, well, no doubt I shall be more successful,' remarked Shrive, with that confidence which was always so inspiring. 'Tell me, did you notice anything strange or unusual in your curate's manner prior to this particular Tuesday?'

'No — no, nothing . . . At least . . . Yes, there was one small thing . . . '

'Pray do not omit anything, however insignificant it may appear to you,' said my friend.

'It was a remark he made — at tea,' said Mr. Willingham. 'He asked whether I thought the night would be dark and if the wind was likely to change.'

'H'm . . . The night was in reality moonlit?'

'Only for a short period. During the time I saw Bimbury performing his extraordinary dance upon the lawn . . . '

'Indeed? Up to then and afterwards it was dark?'

'Yes.'

'And what direction was the wind?'

'Blowing inland from the sea.'

'It did not, in fact, change?'

Mr. Willingham shook his head and looked a little bewildered. I confess that I, too, was unable to understand Shrive's interest in the weather.

'One more question,' said my friend, 'and then I should like to have a look at the lawn where your curate indulged in his Terpsichorean exercises. When you looked out of your window and, later, when you went down and discovered that he had disappeared, did you hear any sound?'

'No, nothing.'

Shrive smiled and rubbed his lean hands together.

'Let us inspect the lawn,' he said.

The vicarage stood on the top of the cliff, facing the sea. Beyond the lawn was a thick hedge and then a wide stretch of coarse grassland to the cliff edge, with an almost sheer drop of two to three hundred feet to the beach below.

Lattimer Shrive made a careful examination of the lawn and was shown the exact spot on which the Reverend Timothy Bimbury had last been seen. This was near a straggling shrubbery that divided the garden of the vicarage from the grounds of another house that we could see among some trees a short distance away.

'Who is your neighbour?' asked Shrive, contemplating this habitation with interest.

'A — er — gentleman named Harkness,' answered Mr. Willingham. 'A very charming man and a bachelor like myself. He bought the house about a year ago. A most desirable addition to our — er — little community.'

Shrive seemed very interested in Mr. Harkness. He asked a number of questions that seemed to me to be totally irrelevant and then insisted on inspecting the strip of grassland between the hedge and the clifftop.

'A remarkably fine view,' he said, staring out to sea. 'That is a very fine yacht moored out there.'

'Yes,' agreed the vicar. 'It belongs to an invalid friend of Mr. Harkness's who visits him periodically. His doctor has ordered him sea air, and he lives on board, spending his time cruising about the coast.'

'An excellent way of spending one's time, too,' remarked Shrive. 'I think I have seen all I want to here. I shall, with your permission, take a stroll through this really lovely village and turn over one or two ideas in my mind that have occurred to me. You needn't come, Jarvis. You had better make up some of that sleep of which I deprived you this morning.'

I did not sleep. My mind was too actively engaged in trying to find a solution to this queer affair. Shrive had undoubtedly evolved a theory, though what he had based it on I could not possibly imagine.

He returned at half-past four in the best of spirits, and ate an enormous tea of hot buttered toast.

'Well,' he remarked, sipping his third cup of strong tea. 'I must thank you, Mr. Willingham, for introducing to my notice a really unique little problem. Simple as it was . . . '

'Simple!' I exclaimed. 'Do you mean that you have solved it, Shrive?'

'I hope to present you with a complete solution tonight,' he said, 'provided that . . . '

'Provided what?' I demanded.

'Provided there is no moon and the wind does not change,' he answered.

★   ★   ★

It was a dark night, but not so dark that it was impossible to see, and a stiff wind blew in from the sea.

Lattimer Shrive and I crouched in the shelter of some bushes at the edge of the vicarage lawn. We had taken up our positions there shortly before midnight, and my companion had given me strict injunctions not to talk or make the slightest noise.

I had no idea what we were waiting for. Shrive can be very trying at times, and no amount of questioning would make him divulge the reason for our vigil.

So far as I was concerned I could make nothing of it. What the darkness of the night, and the direction of the wind, had to do with the extraordinary behaviour and disappearance of the Reverend Timothy Bimbury I could not imagine. Long association with Lattimer Shrive, however, had convinced me that there was always a logical reason for any action he took, and so I waited as patiently as I could.

It was a long vigil. The breeze whispering in the trees and bushes and the murmur of the surf on the beach below were the only sounds that reached us.

I had just looked at the luminous dial of my watch, and seen that it was almost one o'clock, when Shrive's hand closed on my arm. Another sound had crept into the night — the faint whispering of voices. It came from beyond the shrubbery in which we were hidden. Something vaguely white seemed to hover in the air above our heads, and a man's voice said urgently: 'There it is! Catch it.'

Shrive raised his hand to his lips and a whistle shrilled out.

'Come on, Jarvis,' he cried, and plunged through the shrubbery into the garden of Mr. Harkness's house. As he did so, the white beam of a searchlight cut a bright path through the darkness, wavered to and fro above our heads, and focused on a large object that was floating in the air.

'Shrive,' I cried in amazement. 'Shrive . . . It's a *kite* . . . '

He took no notice. He was striding towards three men dimly visible in the reflected light of the beam.

'Mr, Harkness, I believe?' he said to the tallest of the trio. 'I should advise you not to make any attempt to escape. The place is surrounded . . . '

'This is an outrage,' snarled Harkness. 'I shall . . . '

'You will tell us what you have done with the Reverend Timothy Bimbury,' cut in my friend, sternly. 'Jarvis, there is a long string depending from that kite. Might I trouble you to pull the contraption down? Be very careful, my dear fellow, or you may damage the consignment of French perfumes which the kite is carrying . . . '

'When you propounded your little problem,' said Lattimer Shrive, as we all sat in Mr. Willingham's study — including the Reverend Timothy Bimbury, whom we had found, bound and gagged, in a top room in Harkness's house — 'the first thing that struck me was the extreme improbability that Mr. Bimbury was actually dancing when you saw him on the lawn. Such an absurd action on his part could only be accounted for by the fact that he had suddenly gone mad. But, if he was not dancing, what was he doing? From Mr. Willingham's description of his movements it seemed to me that he might, possibly, be chasing something that was eluding him. The little runs and sudden leaps suggested this as a plausible theory. If this was the case, then the 'something' must have been above him, in the air. It could not have been anything connected with an aeroplane because there had been no sound. There remained a balloon, some sort of bird, or a kite. The fact that he had been so interested in the direction of the wind ruled out the second of these three possibilities and I was left with the choice of a balloon or a kite.'

Shrive paused and took a sip of the tea at his elbow.

'At this point in my conjectures,' he continued, 'I learned that the house next to this was inhabited by a Mr. Harkness, who had a friend who spent his time cruising around the coast in a large yacht. The significance of this struck me immediately. If these two, Harkness and his friend, were engaged in smuggling on a large scale, it provided a solution not only for the disappearance of Mr. Bimbury — if he had accidentally discovered what was going on — but for the use to which a kite or balloon could have been put. With the wind blowing inland, a kite flown from the yacht and attached to a measured length of cord would reach directly over the grounds of Harkness's house and, allowing for the height of the cliff, would not be very high up. A fair-sized kite, too, would be capable of carrying a considerable amount of contraband goods, if they were of the small variety like perfumes; and, flown on several nights when the weather was suitable, could be the means of unloading a very large cargo in complete immunity from detection. With a long cord depending from the kite, to which something had been attached to render it visible to the people waiting to receive it, it could easily be pulled down, its cargo unloaded, and the kite re-launched into the air and pulled back to the boat.

'When I had evolved this theory I went down to the village and had a word with the police. I received confirmation of what I already knew: that a very large quantity of French perfumes was being smuggled into the country in some manner which could not be traced. I suggested that a trap should be set, with the result you all know.'

'I owe you a very large debt of gratitude, Mr. Shrive,' said the Reverend Timothy Bimbury. 'I had seen the kite on previous nights and guessed what was happening. I should have mentioned it to the vicar but, foolishly, I wanted to do the thing off my own bat. I was chasing the tassel thing on the end of that cord, which had drifted over the vicarage garden, when Harkness and his friends set upon me. I don't remember any more until I came to, to find myself bound and gagged, in the room in which you found me.'

'A really amazing achievement, Mr. Shrive,' said the Reverend Oswald Willingham. 'I really cannot conceive how you managed to deduce the truth from such a paucity of data. A truly remarkable piece of reasoning.'

'A mere bagatelle,' murmured Lattimer Shrive modestly. 'Jarvis, my dear fellow, might I trouble you to brew another pot of this very excellent tea . . . ?'

The Extraordinary Problem of the Eccentric Lodger

*as related by Nelson Jarvis, F.R.I.B.A.,
to Gerald Verner*

If my memory is not at fault — a matter, by the way, which forms the basis for continuous argument between myself and my partner — it was only on two occasions that I was directly instrumental in bringing to the notice of my friend Lattimer Shrive one of those bizarre little problems that his keen analytical brain delights to unravel.

The first of these was the fantastic affair of the Impudent Taxi-driver, which involved such an illustrious personage that I am prohibited from revealing the true facts. It is enough to say that for his delicate handling of this intricate case, Lattimer Shrive was offered a knighthood, but he refused the honour.

'The very idea of such a thing is abhorrent to me, Jarvis,' he said, when I remonstrated with him. 'As a reward for such small talents as I possess I seek no personal aggrandizement. *This* has touched me more than the conferring of a title could ever do.' He held up his left hand, on the middle finger of which sparkled an emerald ring. I felt rebuked by this evidence of his native simplicity, and apologized.

The second case was the strange business that I am about to relate. It was first brought to my attention by Mrs. Gumption, a very worthy and respectable person who is responsible for keeping my office clean. I had, for several evenings, been working later than is my usual habit in order to complete the plans for a block of flats on which I was engaged. My partner, good fellow that he is, is so afraid that I shall do more than my fair share of the office work that he goes to the opposite extreme and tries to prevent my doing anything at all, so that my only chance is to wait until he has gone home for the day when I wish to do something important. I was on the point of going home on this particular evening when Mrs. Gumption, who had been clattering about in my partner's office, appeared at the communicating door and accosted me nervously:

'Excuse me, sir, for h'intrudin', but could I 'ave a word with you?'

'Certainly, Mrs. Gumption,' I said pleasantly.

'It's about my sister-in-law, sir,' she said. ' 'er wot keeps the lodgin' 'ouse in Coram Street. She's bin 'avin' a bit of trouble an' I thought maybe, p'raps, you could advise 'er, sir . . . ?'

'What sort of trouble?' I asked.

'Over one of 'er lodgers, sir,' answered Mrs. Gumption. 'A feller called 'armer . . . '

'Do you mean that he's behind with his rent . . . ?'

'Oh, no, sir,' she broke in, shaking her grey head. 'It ain't nothin' like that. My sister-in-law knows 'ow to deal with them sort. It's 'is be'aviour that's botherin' 'er, sir.'

'How has Mr. — er — Harmer been misbehaving?' I inquired.

'Ever since 'e came there, which is five weeks come next Monday,' said Mrs. Gumption, ' 'e's bin carryin' on somethin' chronic. Why 'e took such a dislike to poor Mr. Wilkinson I'm sure I couldn't say, fer a quieter feller you couldn't wish for, but take a dislike to 'im 'e did, from the word 'go' as you might say. Some of the things wot 'e chalked on 'is door — poor Mr. Wilkinson's, I mean — was shameful an' disgustin', an' that's all you could say of 'em . . . '

'Chalked on his door?' I exclaimed. 'You don't mean the — er — well, the sort of things that — er . . . ?'

'That's just wot I do mean, sir,' declared Mrs. Gumption. 'An' that ain't the worst of it, no, not by a long way. The night afore last poor Mr. Wilkinson comes 'ome to find an 'orrible smell in the passage, an' wot do you think it was, sir?'

'I've no idea,' I replied.

'A dead cat,' said Mrs. Gumption, impressively. 'Tied on the 'andle of 'is door it were, an' smellin' somethink hawful.'

'Good gracious!' I cried. 'This man — er — Harmer must be a little mad.

What reason can he have for this animosity towards Mr. Wilkinson?'

'I don't see as 'ow he can 'ave any,' said Mrs. Gumption. 'Yer see, sir, they ain't never met.'

'Never met?'

'No, sir. You see Mr. 'armer works all night — 'e's night watchman at the Royal Cinema round the corner — and Mr. Wilkinson's out all day. 'E works at Finnimore's, the builders — a clerk 'e is. Mr. 'armer's in bed an' asleep when 'e goes in the mornin', and 'e's gorn out afore Mr. Wilkinson gets back at night.'

'A regular Box and Cox,' I remarked, but Mrs. Gumption quite evidently didn't understand the allusion. 'I should advise your sister-in-law to get rid of Harmer as soon as possible.'

'She's givin' 'im notice come this Sunday,' said Mrs. Gumption. 'But I was wonderin' if she didn't oughter tell the police . . . ?'

'I hardly think that it's a case for the police,' I answered, 'unless, of course, he should make any serious trouble.'

She thanked me and I left her to

continue her cleaning. I intended calling on Lattimer Shrive before going home and I took a taxi to Albany. His Irish housekeeper, Mrs. Bedlow, announced me in her usual sepulchral voice and I discovered Shrive, like Mr. Venus, 'floating his powerful mind in tea'. He offered me a cup of the almost black brew, which I declined.

After we had chatted for some time, it occurred to me that he might be interested to hear about the eccentric lodger, and I related what Mrs. Gumption had told me. He listened with that quiet intentness which always makes it a pleasure to tell him anything.

'A delightful little problem, Jarvis,' he remarked, when I had finished. 'There are, as you have already foreseen, of course, quite a number of interesting possibilities.'

I was forced to confess that they had not occurred to me.

'The only conclusion I came to was that the man must be mad,' I said.

'That is the obvious one, of course,' agreed Shrive. 'But there are several explanations for this extraordinary conduct on

96

the part of Harmer, one of which is distinctly fascinating — distinctly fascinating.'

I begged him to tell me what he meant, but he shook his head, 'Not now, my dear fellow,' he said, 'but if you hear anything further from the excellent Mrs. Gumption, I should esteem it a very great favour if you would let me know at once.'

★ ★ ★

It was on the following Monday evening that Lattimer Shrive's prophecy bore fruit. Mrs. Gumption arrived at the office in a state of great breathlessness.

'Oh, Mr. Jarvis,' she panted. 'I was 'opin' that I'd be in time ter catch yer, sir. I run all the way from the bus stop. 'E's gorn, sir — Mr. 'armer.'

'Well, well, Mrs. Gumption,' I said. 'That solves the problem, doesn't it? Now your sister-in-law will have no more trouble.'

'Trouble!' cried Mrs. Gumption. 'Lawks o' mercy, sir, ain't there though? 'armer's 'opped off with the weekend takin's from the cinema — nigh on four 'undred quid

— an' the perlice is after 'im. They're round at me sister-in-law's now.'

'What is your sister-in-law's address?' I interrupted, with, I'm afraid, scant ceremony, for I had suddenly remembered my promise to Shrive.

She gave an address in Coram Street.

'You go back there, my good woman,' I said, hastily. 'I will follow you in a few minutes, and maybe I can be of some assistance.'

'I'm sure Sarah'll be very grateful, sir,' she said, 'bein' at her wits' end and that worried . . . '

'Naturally, naturally,' I said, and diplomatically edged her out.

I was lucky enough to find an empty taxi at once and drove to Albany. When I arrived, Lattimer Shrive was examining some documents with the aid of a powerful lens, but he put them away immediately he heard what I had to say.

'Excellent, Jarvis, excellent,' he remarked, rubbing his hands. 'I felt sure there would be developments. I trust that you kept the taxi cab waiting?'

I nodded, and a few seconds later we

were speeding towards Bloomsbury.

We found Mrs. Gumption and her sister-in-law, a gaunt woman whom she introduced as Mrs. Blocker, talking to a pleasant-faced, slightly bald man, who turned out to be Mr. Wilkinson, the object of the missing Harmer's unaccountable dislike.

'I always thought there'd be trouble with that feller,' declared Mr. Wilkinson, pursing his lips. 'If you ask me he 'ad a screw loose somewhere.'

'I understand,' said Lattimer Shrive, 'that you can suggest no reason why you should have been singled out for his — er — extraordinary and unpleasant attentions?'

'No reason at all, sir,' said Wilkinson, shaking his head. 'I never met the feller . . . '

'That's right,' confirmed Mrs. Blocker. 'An' I wish I 'and't, neither. My 'ouse 'as always bin respectable, as anyone 'ull tell you . . . '

'I am quite sure of that, madam,' said my friend with that courtliness that charmed all hearts. 'Are the police still on the premises?'

'Left five minutes afore you got 'ere, sir,' answered Mrs. Gumption. 'But that there Inspector Martin said as 'ow he might be comin' back . . . '

'Ah, Martin, eh?' said Shrive, giving me a significant look from the eye that bears such a striking likeness to the late Mr. Gladstone's. 'So he's in charge of this business? I wonder, Mrs. Blocker, whether I might be permitted to inspect the room occupied by Harmer?' Mrs. Blocker consented and led the way upstairs. Harmer's room on the second floor was small and barely furnished, and was next door to that occupied by Mr. Wilkinson.

Harmer had gone without taking any of his personal belongings. His few toilet articles still littered the top of the rickety chest of drawers, and a spare suit of clothes hung over the back of a chair. Shrive crossed the threshold after a minute or so and began a meticulous examination of the room. With the aid of a powerful lens he inspected the bed, the washstand, the missing man's hairbrushes and comb, and even the dust in the fire-grate. Several times I saw him smile to himself, and twice he carefully collected some minute object and put it away in one of the little transparent envelopes which he always carried for this purpose.

'Well, well,' he remarked at last. 'I think that's all we can learn here. Might I trouble you, Jarvis, to oblige me with a pencil? Thank you.' He took out of his pocket an old envelope, ripped it open, and began to sketch rapidly, using the top of the chest of drawers for a table. He eyed the result thoughtfully for a moment, added a couple of swift strokes, and turned to Mrs. Blocker.

'Does that suggest to your mind anyone you know?' he inquired, holding out the sketch to her. She looked at it and gave a gasp of surprise.

'Why, it's Mr. 'armer, sir,' she exclaimed. 'When did you see 'im, sir . . . ?'

'I have never seen him,' answered Shrive, calmly. 'That sketch is purely the result of observation and deduction.'

'But this is amazing, Shrive,' I declared in astonishment, looking at the masterly portrait of a bearded man with a mop of unruly hair which my friend had executed with a few clever pencil strokes. 'How in the world did you know . . . ?'

'I'm afraid I cannot go into that now, my dear fellow,' he broke in. 'It was really quite simple, I assure you. Have you a telephone in the house, Mrs. Blocker?'

'No, sir,' said the landlady, 'but there's a call-box on the corner just a few yards away.'

'Thank you,' said Shrive. 'If you will excuse me, there is a call I wish to make. No, Jarvis, you need not trouble to come. I shall only be a few minutes.'

He was gone for less than five, and he had only just returned when there was a tremendous knock on the front door to herald the arrival of Inspector Martin.

'Mr. Shrive . . . and Mr. Jarvis, too,' said the Inspector as soon as he saw us. 'I didn't expect to find you two gentlemen here. Not your cup o' tea, Mr. Shrive. Just a plain open an' shut case. It's only a question of time before we pull in Harmer . . . '

'Do you really think so, my dear Martin?' said Lattimer Shrive with an inscrutable smile.

'Can't get far,' said the Inspector confidently. 'We've got his description circulated, an' every police officer in the country is on the lookout for him.'

'I have every reason to believe that such methods will prove completely unsuccessful,' remarked Lattimer Shrive quietly. 'Might I inquire for whom the police are searching?'

Inspector Martin looked as completely astonished as I felt.

'Why . . . Why for Harmer, of course, Mr. Shrive,' stammered the Inspector.

'Then allow me to inform you,' said Shrive calmly, 'that you are wasting your time. *There is no such person.*'

'Come now, Mr. Shrive,' said Inspector Martin. 'You can't really mean that, you know. Both these women have seen and spoken to Harmer, and so has the manager of the Royal Cinema where he was employed as night watchman.'

'They have seen and spoken to a person *who called himself Harmer,*' interrupted Lattimer Shrive, 'who, with the aid of a wig, a beard, and the careful use of greasepaint, cleverly built up the personality of an individual who did not exist, and even went to the length of carrying out a series of petty annoyances against himself to make that personality more convincing. Allow me to introduce you to the *real* Mr. Harmer!'

And he pointed at Wilkinson, who stared at him with dropped jaw for a second and then, swinging round, made a desperate bolt for the staircase. But Inspector Martin, recovering from his surprise at Shrive's revelation, was too quick for him.

'No you don't,' he panted gruffly, grabbing him by the collar and one arm. 'You're coming with me.'

'You'll find the stolen money concealed somewhere in his room, Martin, I've no doubt,' remarked Shrive. 'I feel in need of tea and toast, Jarvis. Let us return to Albany and get Mrs. Bedlow to supply us with both . . .'

* * *

'I am extremely grateful to you, Jarvis, for bringing to my notice such an interesting little problem,' said Lattimer Shrive, between gulps of tea and mouthfuls of hot buttered toast an hour later. 'Simple as it was, there were a great many points of interest.'

'I still have no idea how you managed to discover the truth,' I said.

He looked at me, chuckled, and rubbed his lean hands. 'When you first mentioned the matter,' he said, 'it struck me that, unless he was mad, all these petty annoyances which the supposed Harmer was inflicting on his fellow lodger, Wilkinson, could only have one object — to draw attention to himself. But for what reason? You then informed me that Harmer had robbed the Royal Cinema of the weekend takings and disappeared. Now a man who is contemplating a robbery would be the last man to draw attention to himself. On the contrary, he would wish to remain as inconspicuous as possible. I then remembered that he and Wilkinson had never been seen together, and that while Harmer worked all night, Wilkinson worked all day — a curious Box and Cox arrangement that suggested the possibility that these two might very well be one. In the light of this theory, Harmer's behaviour towards Wilkinson became understandable. It accentuated the difference between them *psychologically*, as well as physically. It was a very ingenious scheme on Wilkinson's part to create a mythical personality that could be made to disappear instantly on the removal of a wig and a beard and a change of clothes. I had already reached this conclusion before ever we entered the house in Coram Street,' he continued. 'An inspection of the room occupied by Harmer confirmed it. I found traces of false hair from a wig and also one or two hairs to which a minute quantity of spirit gum still adhered, which suggested a beard. I ventured to make a sketch of *Wilkinson* with the addition of a good crop of hair and a beard, and Mrs. Blocker instantly recognized it as *Harmer*. A telephone call to Finnimore's, the builders, revealed the fact that no one of the name of Wilkinson, or answering to his description, worked there, which added the final confirmation that I needed.'

The telephone bell rang. He crossed the room to answer it. After a few seconds' conversation, he returned to his easy chair.

'That was Martin,' he said. 'The stolen money was found in a tin box in the chimney of Wilkinson's room. Well, well, that's that, my dear fellow. What do you say to a game of chess?'

I agreed, though I knew Shrive would win. He always does.

Death at the Microphone

The author wishes to make it quite clear that although there are various terms and technical references connected with Broadcasting House in this story which are accurate, they are employed solely to make the narration convincing, and are in no way intended as a portrayal in characterization of such positions on the B.B.C. staff with which the story is concerned. All the characters are fictitious and are not intended to refer to any living person.

1

The Broadcast Murder

A taxi swerved into the kerb and came to a halt outside the entrance to the huge building of white stone at the beginning of Portland Place that housed the activities of the British Broadcasting Corporation.

A big man got heavily out and dropped several coins into the willing and somewhat dirty palm of the driver. The taxi jerked away from the kerb, and the late fare, after a moment's pause, crossed the strip of pavement, wet and shining in the falling drizzle, and entered the vestibule.

At the reception desk in the right-hand corner of the big hall the commissionaires, who replaced the daytime receptionists, were checking over the items of studio accommodation for the evening programmes.

Ex-Superintendent Rawlings, late of the C.I.D., strolled towards them.

'Good evening, sir?' one of the men looked up enquiringly.

'Good evening,' said Rawlings pleasantly. 'I'm broadcasting a talk tonight — '

'What name, sir?'

'Rawlings. Ex-Superintendent Rawlings.'

The commissionaire looked through a sheaf of papers and nodded.

'That's right, sir. National Programme, seven-forty to eight. Studio number sixteen. You're a little early, sir.' He glanced across at the clock. It was barely seven.

'I'm afraid I am,' admitted Rawlings. 'What do I do?'

'You could go up in the listening room and hear some of the other programmes, or the waiting room — '

'Thank you, I'll go to the listening room,' said Rawlings, and the commissionaire pressed a button.

Almost miraculously, as though he had been conjured up out of the air, a page appeared.

'Take this gentleman up to listening room 6a,' ordered the commissionaire, and with a brief nod Rawlings followed the page to a lift.

There were a number of people who did not like Ex-Superintendent George Rawlings, and amongst them was the greater part of his former colleagues at Scotland Yard. He was rather a taciturn man with an abrupt manner of speech and a harsh, metallic voice that could, however, sound very soft and human on occasions — though the occasions were few. His face was big and square and heavily jowled, looking as though it had been hewn out of wood and never quite finished.

His eyebrows were shaggy and almost hid the small, keen eyes that surveyed the world with a hard glitter. His hair was sparse and iron grey; his mouth a thin, straight line; and perhaps because of this, people — judging from outward appearances — called him harsh and cruel. To those law-breakers who owed the loss of their freedom to his efforts, he was, for he had no sympathy with criminals; others who knew him better did not judge so hastily from his rather forbidding exterior. There was one who thought him the kindest of men, but she was his daughter and had every reason to think so, for he was a most indulgent father.

Marion Rawlings was the one bright spot in the ex-superintendent's rather gloomy life. After the death of his wife he had lavished all his affection on the child, and had seen her grow from girlhood to womanhood with pride.

He was thinking of her now as he stepped out of the lift on the seventh floor and entered the tower within which all the studios were built. The listening room was a large apartment, ultra-modern in decoration, with several comfortable chairs facing a loud speaker set on a dais at one end, behind which was an illuminated background depicting a river and skyscrapers.

There were several other people present listening to a march that was being played by a military band in the Birmingham studio. Rawlings sat down and lighted a cigarette. He liked music — military band music in particular — and he smoked and listened contentedly, unaware that the last hour of his life was slowly passing.

Presently the door opened and a good-looking man came over to his side. Rawlings recognized him as the announcer with whom he had rehearsed his talk.

'Will you come with me?' whispered the newcomer. 'It's getting near your time.'

The ex-superintendent nodded and followed him out. The talk studio, from which he was to broadcast, was a small room furnished comfortably with well-filled bookcases, two armchairs and a desk. Except for the microphone which hung above the latter, it might have been a private study.

'Got your script?' asked the announcer.

The ex-superintendent nodded and took from his pocket a wad of manuscript. It was typed on the peculiar paper that the B.B.C. used for all such things, and which was rather like blotting paper in texture; it was used because it did not crackle.

At that moment an elderly man put his head through the partly open door.

'I want you, Henley,' he said. 'A police message has just come through and I want you to broadcast it at once.'

Henley frowned.

'I'm looking after Superintendent Rawlings' talk — ' he began, but the Chief Announcer interrupted him.

'I'll do that,' he said. 'You go and read the message, it's on your table.'

'But — ' protested Henley.

'That is all!' said the other rather sharply.

Henley departed reluctantly and the newcomer turned to Rawlings.

'You've got about ten minutes before you start,' he said. 'When that red light flickers the mike's alive and you start, and for God's sake remember that until the light goes out any sound you make will go out over the air. We had a man giving a talk last week who forgot that and exclaimed, 'Thank Heaven that's done!' as soon as he'd finished, and it was broadcast to millions.'

'I'll remember,' said Rawlings with a smile, and seated himself at the table.

'Feeling nervous?' asked the man as the ex-superintendent took out his hand-kerchief and wiped his face.

'Just a little,' answered Rawlings.

'You'll get over that as soon as you start,' said the Chief Announcer cheerily. 'Your rehearsal went very well; you'll be all right. Don't speak too fast, that's the main thing.' He glanced at his watch. 'I must make arrangements for the prelimi-nary announcement,' he said. 'Well — good luck!' He went out, closing the sound-proof door behind him.

Rawlings spread the typescript of the talk on the desk before him and settled himself for the coming ordeal. Now that it was so near at hand, it seemed an even worse ordeal than he had imagined. The blank face of the microphone stared at him — a dead thing that in a few moments would be alive and sending his words to the homes of millions . . .

It was very still and silent in the studio — a curious deadly silence that was oppressive. It reminded him of the moment in court before the judge pronounced the death sentence. With a hand that was a little unsteady, he reached out to the carafe of water that stood before him and poured a little into a glass. He sipped it and set the glass down again. Surely something had gone wrong? It must be more than ten minutes since he had come into this box-like room. The clock showed him that he was mistaken — there were still four minutes to go before the scheduled time for the talk. As calmly as he could, he waited.

An age seemed to pass before the red light before him flicked on and glowed steadily . . .

★   ★   ★

'I'm sure,' said Mr. Whipple, 'that it will be most interesting — most interesting.'

Inspector Gallers grunted. He was not at all sure that he wanted to listen to this talk given by his ex-colleague Rawlings, but his little neighbour had been so enthusiastic when he had issued his invitation to come in and hear it that he hadn't had the heart to refuse.

'What time is the talk?' he asked.

'Seven-forty,' answered Mr. Whipple, 'on the National wavelength.'

'That's in five minutes,' remarked the inspector, looking at the clock on the mantelpiece, and allowing his eyes to travel from thence to the tray of whisky and soda that stood on a table in Mr. Whipple's cosy little study.

Mr. Whipple saw the glance and hastened to offer a practical reply.

'Help yourself, Inspector,' he said hospitably. 'Ex-Superintendent Rawlings is speaking on the Sussex Murder Mystery. I've no doubt you remember it, a most peculiar and extraordinary crime.'

'I remember it,' said Gallers, holding up the fizzy drink he had mixed. 'Well, here's your very good health, Mr. Whipple.' He drank half of it and carried the remainder back to his chair.

'That's the concert just ending,' said

Mr. Whipple as the selection that was being played came to its crashing finale. 'We shan't have long to wait now.'

There was a moment's silence and then the announcer's voice spoke clearly and distinctly:

'This is the National Programme from London. We have in the studio tonight ex-Superintendent Rawlings of the C.I.D, who will give the first talk in the series 'Unsolved Crimes'. Superintendent Rawlings' subject is the Sussex Murder Mystery, and he is particularly qualified to speak about this crime because he was in charge of the investigations at the time. Ex-Superintendent Rawlings!'

The announcer's voice ceased and was followed by a preliminary cough; then the rather grating tones of Rawlings reached their ears:

'Most of you will remember the case which the newspapers called the 'Sussex Murder Mystery',' he began. 'A woman called Bedwell was killed in her house at Rayden. She was found strangled on her bed and — '

The voice stopped suddenly and there

came a startled exclamation from the loudspeaker.

'What — ' came Rawlings' voice again, shrill with fear, and then the unmistakable sound of a shot. It was followed instantly by a groan, the thud of a closing door and — silence!

'Good God, what could have happened?' cried Gallers, springing to his feet.

'Something pretty serious, apparently,' said Mr. Whipple, his face grave. 'That was undoubtedly a pistol shot.'

'But he can't have been shot in Broadcasting House!' muttered the inspector. 'It's — listen!' He stopped abruptly and held up his hand. The announcer was speaking, not in his usual careful way but hurriedly and shakily.

'We must apologize to listeners, but an accident has occurred in the studio occupied by ex-Superintendent Rawlings,' he said. 'The talk he was to give will have to be abandoned, and a programme of gramophone records will be broadcast almost immediately.'

The agitated voice stopped.

'I wonder what really happened?' said Mr. Whipple curiously.

'I don't know,' replied Gallers, 'but I think that we, in company with millions of other people, have just heard a murder being committed!'

2

Harris Takes Charge

Major Marshland, the Administrative Controller of the B.B.C., sat at his desk wading through the pile of papers in front of him. His brows were drawn together in a frown and he was not in the best of tempers, for he had had, owing to pressure of work, to cancel a dinner engagement and work late, which did not meet with his complete approval. A tall, white-haired man, he looked exactly what he was — a retired soldier — and somehow seemed out of place in the ultra-modern surroundings which constituted his office. He scrawled his illegible signature at the foot of a long report and wearily reached for another.

As his hand touched it, the house

telephone at his side rang softly, and with a very soldier-like exclamation he picked up the instrument.

'Hello?' he growled irritably.

A scared voice came faintly over the wire.

'This is Henley, sir,' it said. 'Something dreadful has happened. Will you come to studio number sixteen at once?'

'What's that? What's that?' barked the major. 'What's all this nonsense? What the devil do you mean by disturbing — '

'It's very serious,' broke in the voice of the announcer. 'Ex-Superintendent Rawlings has been shot — '

'Shot!' Major Marshland's face, always florid, went purple, and he gasped heavily like a newly-landed fish. 'Shot? What the devil do you mean?'

'He was shot while he was broadcasting his talk, sir,' went on the voice of Henley. 'It looks like murder.'

'Murder!' The major looked as if he was going to have a stroke. 'In Broadcasting House? Nonsense, nonsense!'

'It's true all the same, sir,' said Henley.

'All right, all right, I'll come at once!

Studio number sixteen, did you say?' And then, in milder tones: 'I say, Henley, keep this as quiet as possible.'

He jabbed the telephone back on its rack and rose to his feet in one concerted movement. With his handkerchief he mopped his face and went over to the door. Making his way quickly to the main entrance hall, he ran into the house-superintendent just coming out of his office.

'I'm glad you're here, sir,' said the latter, his face white and worried. 'This is a dreadful business! I've been on to Scotland Yard and they're sending a detective and a police sergeant at once.'

'Are you sure it's necessary?' growled the major. 'It means a lot of unpleasant publicity.'

'I'm afraid we can't avoid that, sir,' broke in the superintendent. 'It's undoubtedly a case of murder; I've seen the body.'

The major clicked his teeth impatiently.

'Yes, yes, but — good God!' A thought struck him suddenly. 'In the middle of his talk, was it?'

'He'd only just begun, sir,' answered

the superintendent.

'I mean the — the — mike was live?' snapped Marshland, and the other nodded. 'Then — then the whole thing was broadcast — 'The Major left the sentence unfinished and gasped.

'Yes I'm afraid it was broadcast all right, sir,' said the house superintendent grimly. 'They've started ringing up already.'

They had been making their way to the lift while speaking, and Marshland lapsed into gloomy silence as they were whisked up to the seventh floor. Outside Studio sixteen they found a little group standing by the half-open door. Henley, the announcer, rather shaky and white-faced, came forward as they approached.

'This is a terrible business, sir — ' he began nervously, and the major glared at him.

'Of course it is!' he snapped. 'What's the good of everybody saying that? What have you done about it?'

A tall, thin man detached himself from the group by the door and came forward.

'I took charge, sir,' he said smoothly. 'There's no doubt that Superintendent

Rawlings was shot. I've made certain that he is quite dead and I've kept everybody out of the studio until the police have seen the body.'

Marshland grunted; his red face was worried and anxious. This was a situation that he felt was beyond him. It had no precedent and therefore he was at sea. Soaked in routine, he was completely at a loss when anything happened outside the normal run.

'Well,' he said to the studio manager, who had just finished speaking, 'I suppose we can't do anything until the police have finished their investigations.'

He went up to the partly open door and peered into the small room beyond. He stared for a moment at the figure that sprawled across the desk, and although he had seen death in many forms during his service in the army he shivered. This was not the death of battle, but a more sinister thing. This had been done by a creeping enemy that killed and vanished. An unknown enemy . . .

He turned away quickly, and as he did so a man came hurrying along the corridor. Marshland recognized him as a messenger from the telephone room.

'Excuse me, sir,' he panted, 'but Miss Rawlings is on the telephone.'

The Major turned to the house superintendent.

'You speak to her, Gilmore,' he said. 'Switch the call through to Mr. Gilmore's office, will you?'

The messenger saluted and hurried away, followed by the house superintendent. The major mopped his face.

'How many people in the building know about this?' he asked, turning to Henley.

'Very few, sir,' answered the announcer. 'Of course, they know in the control room; they heard the noise of the shot.'

Marshland frowned and then looked at the studio manager.

'Well, we can't do more until the police come,' he muttered. 'You'd better see that no one is allowed to leave this floor. Station a man at each end of the corridor and tell them to make some excuse to anyone who wants to leave.'

The Studio Manager, a man named

McGrath, nodded, and turned to the other two men behind him.

'You attend to that, will you?' he said, and they hurried away to take up their posts.

Marshland went down to the reception hall, and as he reached it met Gilmore coming out of his office.

'Miss Rawlings is on her way, sir,' he said. 'She's very upset.'

The Administrative Controller pulled his nose in annoyance.

'Good God! Aren't things bad enough without having a crying woman about the place?' he rasped. 'Couldn't you stop her?'

'I tried,' answered the house superintendent, 'but she insisted on coming.'

'Oh well, it can't be helped,' growled the major. 'I wonder how long the police will be?'

The police arrived five minutes later. The man in charge was a thick-set individual with a bristling moustache, who introduced himself as Detective-Inspector Harris. He had brought with him a sergeant and a police doctor.

Marshland rapidly related what had happened, and Harris rubbed at his moustache with a stubby hand.

'I suppose you've no idea who fired the shot?' he asked.

Marshland shook his head irritably.

'Not the least idea,' he answered. 'Of course I haven't — otherwise I should have told you.'

'I'd like to go up to the studio where the crime was committed at once, sir,' said the Scotland Yard man. 'I suppose nobody's touched anything?'

'Nobody has been allowed to go in!' declared the major. 'Also I have arranged that nobody on that floor has been allowed to leave it since the man was killed.'

The inspector nodded approvingly.

'Good!' he said. 'Then we'll go up, sir.'

When they reached the seventh floor they found the corridor outside the fatal studio crowded. An outside dance band had just finished its broadcast and the bandsmen were standing about in little groups and chatting in subdued tones of the tragedy that had just reached their ears. McGrath, the Studio Manager, who was trying to pacify the excited band leader, muttered an excuse as he caught sight of Marshland and the others, and came over to them.

'I'm having the deuce of a job to prevent them leaving,' he said with a worried frown, when the Administrative Controller had introduced him to Inspector Harris. 'They're due at the Colodrome in half an hour and they're naturally annoyed. What can we do about it?'

'I'm afraid we can't do anything about it, sir,' said the inspector. 'Nobody who was on this floor at the time the shot was fired must leave until after I have completed my preliminary investigations.'

'Somebody had better phone through to the theatre and explain what has happened,' suggested Marshland. 'I've no doubt that under the circumstances the time of their turn can be altered. That's where it happened,' he added in a low voice, jerking his head towards the half-open door of the talk studio.

The police inspector went over and, standing on the threshold, looked into the tiny room. Then he entered and stared down at the dead man. Rawlings had fallen face downwards across the desk, one arm doubled up beneath him, the other hanging limply by his side. His grey hair was stained with blood and there was more blood on the polished woodwork of the table on which his body rested. Harris made no effort to touch the still figure, but turned to his sergeant who was standing by his side.

'You see his position?' he said under his breath. 'He was sitting with his back to the door.'

The sergeant nodded.

'Yes, I noticed that, sir,' he said.

The Scotland Yard man grunted.

'Before we go any further we'd better let the doctor see him,' he said.

He looked across to the doorway and scowled as he saw the sea of curious faces that filled the opening. Going over, he called the name of the doctor he had brought with him; and when that individual had forced his way in, he rapped an order to the sergeant. The crowd melted away as the man carried out his instructions, and the door was closed.

'That's better,' grunted Harris, coming back to the desk. 'Now then, doctor.'

The police surgeon set about his examination methodically and unhurriedly. At the expiration of three minutes he looked up from his task.

'The man was shot,' he said. 'The bullet entered the left temple and came out just behind the right ear. It passed through the brain, and death must have been instantaneous.'

'Oh, the bullet came out, did it?' grunted Harris. 'Then it should be here somewhere.' He hunted about and presently paused opposite a portion of the wall by the side of the desk. 'There it is,' he said, pointing to a mark. 'We must have it out.'

'I'll do that, sir,' said the sergeant, who began to probe gently at the broken plaster with the open blade of a knife which he took from his pocket.

'Is there any possibility that it could have been suicide?' asked Harris, addressing the police doctor, and the latter shrugged his shoulders.

'There's a possibility, of course,' he

said. 'It's the type of wound that could quite easily have been self-inflicted, but I should think it was distinctly unlikely that he would have chosen such a moment to do it. Besides which, where is the weapon?'

'I think the weapon is here,' remarked Harris, stooping to a patch of shadow under the desk. 'Yes, this is it,' he grunted, and taking a handkerchief from his pocket he picked the object up. 'Why,' he exclaimed, as he brought it out into the light, 'it's a kid's pistol!'

Looking over his shoulder as he held the weapon in his open palm, the doctor saw that he was speaking the truth. It was a toy revolver of the type that was supposed to fire a blank, and which had the barrel sealed up so as to render it harmless. In this case, however, the end of the barrel had been filed off, with the result that it was now a very formidable weapon indeed, especially as it was one of the larger type.

'There ought to be a law to prohibit the sale of these things,' growled the inspector. 'Anybody can buy them at the moment and a few minutes' work with a file can make them as dangerous as a real revolver.'

'They are real revolvers, to all intents and purposes,' said the doctor. 'Very deadly at short range. The only difference is the sealing of the barrel, which is easily removed.'

Harris grunted and turned as the sergeant straightened up from his probing, holding out a little blob of lead in the palm of his hand.

'Here's the bullet, sir,' he said. 'It hadn't penetrated very far.'

The tiny pellet was about the size of a pea, flattened and shiny on one side where it had struck the surface of the wall. The inspector took it and twisted it about in his fingers.

'There's no doubt that it came from that,' he remarked, holding it up next to the revolver. 'Whoever fired the shot must have done so at very close range; there's not much power behind these things.'

'There was enough to serve the murderer's purpose,' put in the police surgeon grimly.

'I'll have this thing tested for finger-prints,' said Harris, wrapping the weapon up carefully in his handkerchief and stowing it away in his inside breast pocket. 'The next thing we'd better do is to get this poor fellow moved.'

There came a tap at the door.

'See who that is,' he growled, and the sergeant went over. In a few minutes he came back.

'Inspector Gallers would like to speak to you,' he said.

Harris's eyebrows went up. 'Gallers, eh? Bring him in.'

Gallers entered, followed by the small and unobtrusive form of Mr. Whipple.

'Hello, Gallers!' grunted Harris. 'What are you doing here?'

'I was listening in and heard the shot,' explained Gallers, 'and I thought I'd come along. Carry on, Harris, I don't want to interfere. It's more a matter of curiosity than anything else with me.'

'Well, there's enough to be curious about,' said Harris, and he told Gallers and the silent but interested Mr. Whipple what he had discovered so far.

The Missing Manuscript

When the body of the unfortunate ex-detective had been removed, Harris made a careful examination of the studio. He found nothing to afford a clue to the tragedy that had happened there. The murderer had committed his crime without leaving any trace except for the pistol, which was practically valueless as a clue. There were thousands of them in existence and there was no restriction regarding their sale. To trace it to its owner would be an almost impossible task.

The shot had obviously been fired from the door. In the midst of his broadcast, Rawlings must have heard the slight sound made by the murderer as he opened the door, and half-turned — that would account for the bullet having entered the left temple. The killer had then flung the pistol away from him and taken his departure. The questions were, who among the numerous people in that huge building had committed the crime, and for what reason?

Mr. Whipple was intensely interested. The case was unique. The fact that thousands of people had heard the fatal shot lifted it from the ordinary routine of murder. The motive must have been a very urgent one, otherwise the murderer would scarcely have chosen the time that he had.

It seemed to the little man that here might be a possible clue. Had it been absolutely essential that Rawlings should die before he could complete his broadcast talk, or was this merely a coincidence? Was the possible motive to be found in that undiscovered crime at Rayden, which had formed the subject matter for his discourse?

Rather diffidently he offered this suggestion to Gallers, and the inspector pursed his lips.

'I don't see how it could, Mr. Whipple,' he muttered, stroking his chin. 'Still, there may be something in it. It's a pity we don't know what he was going to say.'

'It should be quite easy to find out,' ventured Mr. Whipple. 'These talks are not impromptu. He would have had to prepare a manuscript beforehand and submit it to the B.B.C., and also — '

He broke off in the middle of his sentence, and going over peered through his glasses at the desk.

'What is it?' asked Harris.

'Dear me, it's most extraordinary,' murmured Mr. Whipple, shaking his head. 'Where is the copy of the manuscript? It should be here. Superintendent Rawlings must have had it to read from.' He nodded towards the desk; its neat surface was practically bare. There was no sign of any manuscript.

'There was no manuscript here,' said Harris.

'No?' said Mr. Whipple. 'Dear me! Then unless it was moved by one of the officials here, it must have been taken by the murderer.'

They stared at him.

'We'll soon find out,' growled Harris.

James Henley and the studio manager were sent for, but in answer to the inspector's questions they both shook their heads. Nobody had removed anything from the studio. Henley had been the first to make the discovery and he had immediately called McGrath. Between the time he had heard the shot in the loudspeaker in the listening room at the end of the corridor, and the time he had found Rawlings dead, somebody must have removed the manuscript of the talk — and that somebody could only have been the killer.

After the discovery, the talk studio had not been left unguarded for one moment.

Mr. Whipple gently stroked the bridge of his nose. This disappearance of the manuscript went a long way to suggest that the motive for Rawlings' death was somehow mixed up with the killing of Mrs. Bedwell at Rayden. A copy of that ill-fated talk must be obtained. It seemed likely that the whole mystery would be made clear. No doubt there would be a draft at the dead man's home. He was suggesting this to Gallers when Henley broke in.

'If you want a copy of the talk,' said the announcer, 'I've got one. I'll go and fetch it.'

'There are several copies of talks or readings,' explained McGrath, as he left the studio. 'There's one for the announcer in case the speaker forgets to bring his copy, one for filing purposes, and one in case it is decided to publish the talk later on in *The Listener*.'

'I see,' said Harris. 'So in this case there would be four copies altogether, sir?'

McGrath nodded.

'That's very interesting,' murmured Mr. Whipple. 'Very interesting indeed. If the murderer took this script away in the hope that he was going to — er — destroy anything that — er — Rawlings may have been going to say tonight, he had all this trouble for nothing?'

'Completely,' answered the studio manager with a smile. 'And if he was anybody who was acquainted with the routine of the B.B.C., he would have known that.'

'That's — er — that's what I was thinking,' said Mr. Whipple, 'and it would be as well to — er — to remember that fact, don't you think?'

He turned as the door opened quickly and Henley came in. The announcer was looking a little perturbed and agitated.

'The manuscript's gone!' he blurted

out, as he closed the door behind him. 'I left it on the desk in my room with some other papers, and it's completely disappeared.'

Mr. Whipple's eyes narrowed behind his glasses.

'You're sure of that?' snapped Harris.

'Positive!' declared Henley. 'I searched thoroughly. There's nowhere it could have got mislaid.'

'What about the filing copy?' asked the inspector, turning to McGrath. 'Where is that kept?'

'In the filing room,' answered the studio manager.

'Can you send someone to find it?' went on the Scotland Yard man. 'I've got an idea it won't be there, but we may as well make sure.'

'There should be two copies there,' said McGrath, frowning. 'I'll find out and let you know.'

He went out, and Harris turned to the worried Henley.

'You say your room is at the end of the corridor?' he asked. 'Which end?'

'Near the door leading to the lift,'

answered the announcer.

'Was it from there that you made the preliminary announcement for Rawlings' talk?' went on the inspector, and Henley nodded. 'And after you'd introduced him,' Harris continued, 'you listened to the beginning of the talk and then heard the shot?'

'Yes.'

'How much time elapsed,' asked the inspector, 'between your hearing the shot and finding him dead in here?'

'Less than a minute,' replied the announcer. 'I was staggered for a moment. At first I thought he'd knocked something over, and then when he stopped speaking I rushed out of my room and hurried along to the studio.'

'Was the door open or shut when you got here?' asked Harris.

'It was partly open,' answered the announcer. 'When I saw Rawlings huddled up over the desk I was horrified.' He shivered slightly as he recalled that unpleasant moment.

'What did you do then?' asked Harris.

'I shut the door,' continued Henley, 'and called for McGrath. He came along at once and I showed him what had happened, and then on his instructions I went back to my room and telephoned through to Major Marshland.'

'Did you see anybody in the corridor when you came out of your room after hearing the shot?' said the inspector, after a slight pause.

Henley shook his head.

'Not a soul!' he declared.

'And you heard no sound of retreating footsteps, or anything like that?'

'No.'

'It seems curious to me,' put in Gallers, 'that nobody else heard the shot.'

Henley smiled wryly. 'If it was fired with the door closed,' he said, 'nobody would hear it except through the microphone. All these doors are sound-proof; you could fire a bomb in any of the studios and nobody outside would hear a sound.'

'I see,' muttered the Scotland Yard man. 'How many studios are there on this floor?'

The announcer thought for a moment.

'Five,' he replied, and began ticking them off on the fingers of his hand. 'There's this one, the large studio next door where the band was playing, my own studio — which combines the gramophone studio — and two others which were unoccupied.'

'So the only studios which were occupied when Rawlings was killed,' said Harris, 'were the band studio, this one and your own?'

Henley nodded.

'And I presume,' the inspector went on, 'that it would be impossible for a stranger to reach this part of the building without being seen?'

'Completely impossible,' answered the announcer decisively.

'H'm,' grunted Harris, with puckered brows. 'Well, it's a pretty little problem. At the present moment anybody in Broadcasting House could have committed the crime, so I think our best task is to try and narrow that down.'

At that moment Marshland came in. The Administrative Controller's florid face was a little paler than usual and there was a deep furrow between his rather bushy eyebrows.

'Can you do anything about these band

people?' he growled. 'They're kicking up the devil of a row at being kept hanging about.'

'I don't see why they can't be allowed to go,' said Harris. 'After all, they were broadcasting at the time the murder was committed, so their alibis are pretty strong. I'll have a word with them first, though.'

'Have as many words as you like,' said the Major testily, 'but for God's sake do it now and let's get rid of them!'

'All right,' said the inspector, smiling. He went out into the corridor, followed by Gallers and Mr. Whipple.

The bandsmen were still hanging about, looking bored and ill-tempered, and the Scotland Yard man approached their leader.

'Sorry to have kept you,' he apologized gruffly. 'But you understand that it is my duty and I can't help it. A serious crime has been committed here and it's my business to question everybody who may have been remotely connected with it.'

'Neither I nor my boys could have had anything to do with it,' answered the bandleader sullenly. 'We were playing at the time. It's disgraceful that we should be kept hanging about like this; it may mean a serious loss to us! We are playing at the Colodrome — '

'If you could give me your assurance,' Harris interrupted the excited flow, 'that none of your men left the studio in which you were playing during the broadcast, I don't think I need detain you any longer.'

'You have my assurance for that — ' began the bandleader quickly, and then stopped. 'No, I'm afraid that's not quite right,' he added slowly. 'One of my men did leave the studio for a few moments. He felt faint and wanted to get some air. As we were playing a piano solo at the time I let him go.'

'Which one of your men was that?' asked Harris sharply.

'Ted Liddy,' answered the bandleader, and his face was a little troubled. 'But he wouldn't have had any reason — '

'I should like to put a few questions to him all the same,' broke in Harris.

'He's over there,' said the bandleader, who called to a little man leaning against the wall at the far end of the corridor.

He came forward rather reluctantly, Mr. Whipple thought.

'You want me?' he said ungraciously.

At the sound of his voice Harris started.

'Yes, I think we do want you,' he said significantly, looking keenly at the man in front of him. 'So you call yourself Ted Liddy now, do you?'

'It happens to be my name!' snapped the other.

'Does it?' retorted Harris. 'Since when? I know you — your name's Lew Shale, and you've been 'inside' twice for bur-glary. They used to call you the 'Songbird', and your last stretch was four years for the robbery of Mrs. Radnor's emeralds and — By Jove!' his voice became excited and he slapped his thigh. 'And it was Rawlings who put you away!'

4

The Man in the Band

The little man's wizened face went grey: the fear in his small eyes was unmistakable.

'What are you trying to put over on me?' he cried shrilly. 'I had nothing to do with this thing! I'm going straight now!'

Harris looked sceptical.

'I've heard that tale before,' he grunted. 'That's what they all say. I've never met a crook yet that wasn't going straight.'

'I'm telling you the truth!' said the man called Liddy earnestly. 'I've been going straight now for the last six months.'

'And then you suddenly went all crooked,' said the inspector, nodding. 'I know. Well why did you do it?'

'I didn't do it!' cried Liddy excitedly. 'I didn't know Rawlings was in the building until I heard he was dead.'

There was open disbelief on Harris's face. 'What time did you leave the studio,' he asked, 'when you were feeling faint and came out for some air?'

The little man's trembling hands sought his lips as he tried to remember.

'I'm not sure of the time — ' he began, and the bandleader, who had been listening in silence with a rather worried expression on his face, interrupted him.

'I can tell you that,' he said quickly. 'It

was just before seven-forty.'

'There you are,' said Harris. 'Seven-forty was the time Rawlings started his talk and he was killed a minute after. That's pretty conclusive!'

The fear in Liddy's eyes deepened.

'I swear I didn't do it!' he almost wailed. 'You've got to believe me!'

'It depends whether the jury believe you,' grunted Harris. 'I shall have to detain you on suspicion.'

Liddy began to protest vehemently, and Mr. Whipple shifted uncomfortably.

At that moment McGrath put in an appearance, and by the expression on his face it was obvious that he had important news. Mr. Whipple guessed what he was going to say before he spoke, and his guess proved to be right.

'Those two manuscripts in the filing room,' said the studio manager, 'they've disappeared, too.'

'Well, it doesn't much matter,' said Harris. 'I think we've got our man.'

McGrath looked at him wonderingly.

'That's pretty quick work, Inspector,' he exclaimed. 'Who was it?'

The Yard man jerked his head towards the cringing figure of Liddy.

'That's the fellow,' he replied. 'He's an old 'lag' and it was Rawlings who got him his last stretch. The whole thing's quite clear to me. He knew that Rawlings was going to broadcast here this evening, knew that he would also be in the same building and decided to revenge himself on the man who had brought about his imprisonment.'

'It's a lie!' cried Liddy hysterically. 'It's all lies! You're trying to frame me!'

'That'll do!' snapped Harris sternly. 'You'll have an opportunity of making a statement later. Where's that sergeant of mine?'

He looked round, but the sergeant had not yet returned from seeing the body off the premises, and Harris snorted disgustedly.

'Takes some of them years to do anything!' he muttered. 'Wonder how long he's going to be?'

The sergeant appeared as he finished speaking, calling him. Harris pointed to Liddy.

'I'm detaining this man on suspicion,' he said. 'Take him back with you to Cannon Row and lock him up.'

The sergeant nodded stolidly.

'His name is Lew Shale,' continued the Scotland Yard man. 'They've got his record in R.O. When you get back ask them to look it up and send it to my office.'

Again the sergeant nodded and turned to the little crook.

'Come on!' he said briefly, and with a glance of despair Liddy obeyed.

When they had gone, Harris turned to Gallers.

'Well, that's that!' he said cheerfully. 'Not very difficult after all, eh?'

'I think,' interrupted Mr. Whipple gently, 'that it's more difficult than you imagine.'

The inspector stared at him.

'Oh, you do, eh?' he said gruffly. 'Why?'

'Well,' Mr. Whipple reddened uncomfortably under his gaze. 'If this man Liddy killed Rawlings, how do you account for those — those manuscripts?'

Harris shrugged his shoulders.

'There's no reason why he shouldn't have taken them,' he said. 'For all we know he may have been mixed up with the Rayden case. Perhaps it was he who killed the woman, and there was something in Rawlings' talk that would have given him away.'

'But — but how did he manage to get hold of the manuscripts?' persisted Mr. Whipple. 'It was easy enough to take the one that was in Rawlings's desk at the time he was killed, but — but what about the others? How did he know anything about the filing room? How did he know there would be anyone in the announcer's room? How did he find time to — to take them?'

'I don't know, but I expect we shall find out,' said the inspector. 'Liddy's our man, right enough, I'm sure of it.'

Mr. Whipple said no more, but there was a troubled expression on his face, and at that moment Marshland hurried up.

'I hear you've caught the fellow,' he said. 'Well, I must say I'm very glad, though in any case the publicity's going to be very unpleasant.' He frowned and shook his head. 'I'm afraid the papers 'ull make a huge splash of this affair. The place is swarming with reporters now.'

'You can't expect anything else, sir,' said Inspector Harris. 'After all, this is a front page story.'

A messenger arrived at that moment and said something to him in a low voice. Marshland groaned.

'The dead man's daughter's arrived now,' he said, under his breath. 'I've told them to take her to my office. Do you want to see her?'

'Yes,' said Harris.

'Come along, then,' said the Major, and he was starting for the door leading to the lift when McGrath stopped him.

'What about these band fellows, sir?' he said. 'Can we let them go now?'

The Administrative Controller looked at Harris inquiringly.

'Yes, I think you can let them go,' said the inspector. 'There's no reason why we should detain them any longer. I shall want to see their leader tomorrow, though; his evidence will be necessary. I'd better get the man's name and address.'

'We've got Mr. Lutona's address,' said the Major impatiently. 'They'll give it to you downstairs.'

He continued his way to the lift, followed by Gallers and Mr. Whipple. Outside the door of his office he paused. 'I should say this is going to be an unpleasant interview,' he muttered with his hand on the handle, 'and I must confess I'm not looking forward to it. I'm not used to dealing with crying women.'

His fears on this score were groundless, as he quickly discovered, for the slim girl who turned towards them as they entered showed no traces of tears. In fact, in her outward appearance there was no evidence of grief at all. Her face was a little white but emotionless and she returned Marshland's greeting in a voice that was firm and clear. The Administrative Controller uttered an audible sigh of relief as he pushed forward a chair.

'Please sit down, Miss Rawlings,' he said. 'This is a very dreadful affair and it is utterly beyond me to express my sympathy.'

'Please don't try,' she said calmly. 'No, I'd rather stand, if you don't mind. I'm grateful for your sympathy, but nothing you or anyone can say will do any good.' The quietly spoken words were more poignant than even the wildest sobs could have been.

The sudden tragedy had been a terrible blow to Marion Rawlings, and Mr. Whipple's heart ached for her as he saw the hard glitter in her eyes. Beneath the calmness that she had assumed was a devastating sorrow that only time could soften.

'The reason I hurried here so quickly,' she said, without preliminary, 'is that I think I can provide you with a clue to the murderer.'

She opened her handbag and searched in the interior.

'We've already — ' Harris was beginning, when Mr. Whipple interposed.

'What is this clue, Miss Rawlings?' he asked.

'It's a letter that my father received the day before yesterday,' she answered, taking a crumpled envelope from her bag. 'I wanted him to notify the police about it at the time, but he only laughed. I don't think he took it seriously.' She extracted a single sheet of paper from the envelope and held it out in her gloved hand.

Harris took it, glanced at the brief message and frowned. It read:

'So you're going to give a talk at Broadcasting House are you? Lies and perjury got you your promotion and we haven't forgotten it. This may be the last time you'll be able to speak. Remember April 14th, 1923.'

There was no signature.

'Look at that!' said the inspector, handing it to Gallers.

Mr. Whipple peered over his shoulder.

'Dear me,' he said. 'This is most interesting. I suppose, Miss Rawlings, you have no idea what happened on April the fourteenth, nineteen-twenty-three?'

The girl shook her head, and had opened her lips to speak when Gallers interrupted her.

'I can tell you that, Mr. Whipple,' he said, unexpectedly. 'April the fourteenth, nineteen twenty-three, was the date on which

Arthur Lemming and Jake Morrison were sentenced to ten years for the National Union Bank robbery.'

5

The Echo of a Crime

Mr. Whipple closed the book he had been studying, rose to his feet, and returned it with care to the bookshelf. It was nearly two o'clock and he had just returned home from Broadcasting House. He was most interested in the Rawlings murder, interested and decidedly puzzled, for he was by no means satisfied with Harris's solution of the affair. So far as he could see there were three ends to the case: Lew Shale, the little crook bandsman; Arthur Lemming and Jake Morrison, the bank robbers; and the Rayden Murder case, which had never been solved. The question was which of these three was connected with Rawlings' death. They couldn't all be, unless in some inexplicable way they were mixed up.

The fact that the manuscripts of the ex-superintendent's talk had been stolen seemed to suggest that the Rayden case was at the bottom of the business; but, although Mr. Whipple had just refreshed his memory by reading through an account of the crime in an anthology of unsolved mysteries that he possessed, he could find nothing that appeared helpful. Briefly he went over in his mind again the circumstances surrounding the Bedwell murder.

The dead woman, Mrs. Elizabeth Bedwell, had lived by herself in a small four-room house just outside Rayden. Apparently she had been rather eccentric; the neighbours at the inquest had all testified to this fact. She never went out except to work in the little patch of garden behind the house and apparently had no friends; since she had lived there — a period of five years — she had never received a visitor of any kind. She kept no servants, doing all the work of the little house herself. It was through a patrolling policeman that the crime was discovered. Early one morning when he came on his beat he noticed a slight difference in the aspect of Mrs. Bedwell's house. From a window in the upper storey fluttered the end of a curtain. It was not a startling thing, but it had been raining; and this, together with the fact that Mrs. Bedwell never had a window open, even on clear nights, started the constable thinking.

When later he came round again and noticed that Mrs. Bedwell had not taken in her morning newspapers and bottle of milk, which she usually did every morning at exactly eight, he decided to ring her bell. There was no answer to his summons and he got suspicious. This was on a Saturday morning and there was the possibility, of course, that she might have gone away for the weekend. The constable decided that it was hardly likely she would have done so and left the upper window open. He tried the front door and the back door, but they were both locked.

The police had a traditional respect for the sanctity of the home against invasion of any kind, and this policeman was no exception to the rule. He consulted his sergeant before entering Mrs. Bedwell's house, and when they did so they found the woman lying fully dressed, dead on her bed.

There was no doubt that she had been murdered. The marks of the strangler's fingers were plainly visible on her throat. The doctor who was called in later gave his opinion that she had been dead some twelve and a half hours.

This suggested the time of the crime as being round about eight o'clock on the previous evening. The neighbours were interrogated but none of them had heard or seen anything. It was rumoured that the dead woman kept a considerable sum of money in the house, but if this was true the police found no trace of it. There was a square steel box under the bed, but this was empty, although it had not been forced in any way.

Rawlings, into whose hands the case had been given, worked conscientiously to try and find a solution, but without result. Patient investigation into the dead woman's past had revealed nothing. She had no relations living and neither was there anybody who could supply any information concerning her. Prior to coming to Rayden, she had lived in a small cottage on the outskirts of the New Forest.

A round of the tradespeople who had supplied her with goods brought to light the fact that she had paid for everything she had in cash, though where she obtained her money nobody knew. In fact, Mrs. Bedwell had been as much a mystery in life as she was in death.

The little house was searched from cellar to roof without the vestige of a clue being discovered. There were no fingerprints, and none of the doors or windows had been forced. A possible explanation for the crime was that the rumours of her wealth had got to the ears of a professional burglar and, knowing her habits, he had called on some pretext or other, been admitted, and strangled the woman before she could raise an alarm. The only thing against this theory was the time at which the murder had been committed. It seemed unlikely that a professional thief would have chosen such an early hour. The time depended on the doctor's evidence, and it was not always possible for a doctor to be accurate within an hour or so, particularly in a case of strangulation. She might have been killed much later, and if so the burglary theory was more credible.

Rawlings had done everything that was humanly possible to unravel the mystery, but he had failed, and the case had gone down in the records of Scotland Yard among the few unsolved crimes. It was Rawlings' only failure during his career, and Mr. Whipple wondered whether it had rankled in the superintendent's mind. Had he ever quite given it up, or had he been working patiently to try to wipe out the blot of that failure? Perhaps he had been rewarded for his diligence by discovering some clue that would lead to the identity of the unknown murderer; or alternatively, perhaps he had formed some theory regarding the woman's death which was so near the truth that the murderer had got frightened at the prospect of it being made public. It was possible, but there was one grave stumbling block.

Whether Rawlings had discovered something definite about the Rayden crime, or whether he had only formed a theory, how had the murderer become aware of the fact?

Mr. Whipple leaned back in his chair, removed his glasses and softly stroked his forehead. Perhaps he had talked about his idea or his discovery, if any. Or, the first inkling might have reached the unknown murderer through the manuscript, which he would have had to deliver to the B.B.C. several days before his talk was due, in accordance with their regulations. If this latter supposition was correct, then the killer was someone employed at Broadcasting House.

The little man pursed his lips. It seemed absurd to suppose that this could be the case, and yet there was no real reason why it shouldn't be. Obviously the murderer had been connected with the talk Rawlings had been going to give, otherwise there was no reason why the manuscripts should have disappeared. Supposing the murderer to have been someone in Broadcasting House, how did Lew Shale and the threatening letter come into it? Shale might quite easily be a coincidence, but surely it was stretching the possibilities too far to suppose that the letter that Rawlings had received was one also.

Could there be any connection between Lew Shale and the Rayden murder case, and Arthur Lemming and Jake Morrison? Perhaps either Shale or the two bank robbers had been responsible for the death of Mrs. Bedwell, and perhaps Rawlings had been successful in tracing the connection. But in that case, he surely would have gone to Scotland Yard and placed the information he had acquired in the hands of the police. He wouldn't have broadcast it and so given away his knowledge, thereby offering the criminal or criminals a chance to escape.

'Dear me,' thought Mr. Whipple, 'the whole thing is a horrible mix-up, and it is long past my usual time for going to bed. I shall postpone all further thought until tomorrow.'

★　★　★

When he retired, Superintendent Rawlings had bought a house in Highgate. It was a tiny place, its chief recommendation being that it stood in an unusually large amount of ground, and was situated a considerable distance from any other habitation. The ex-superintendent had been very fond of flowers, and had spent the greater part of his time in the garden, converting it from the weed-choked wilderness it had been when he had taken over the premises to the neat and carefully tended garden it was now.

To this pleasant little house came Mr. Whipple and Inspector Gallers on the morning following the tragedy. It had been Mr. Whipple's suggestion; and Gallers, who was off duty, had reluctantly agreed to accompany him. The inspector had no idea what was at the back of the little man's mind, but his respect for his neighbour's intelligence had considerably increased since the two occasions on which Mr. Whipple had proved himself.

'I am not at all satisfied,' Mr. Whipple had explained. 'It may sound — er — a little presumptive of me to say so, but I really believe that Inspector Harris is — er — well, rather prone to jump to conclusions.'

'You don't think Liddy is the man?' said Gallers.

Mr. Whipple shook his head.

'Frankly, I do not,' he declared. 'It can't do any harm if we make — er — one or two inquiries on our own account.'

Marion Rawlings admitted them, and her pale, drawn face brought a little ache to Mr. Whipple's sensitive heart.

'There was a burglary here last night,' she said listlessly. 'I heard nothing because I had taken a sleeping draught, but when I came down this morning I found a window open and the desk in my father's study disturbed.'

Mr. Whipple blinked at her excitedly.

'Dear me, how very extraordinary!' he said. 'A burglary! Might we — er — might we see the room?'

'Of course,' she answered, and showed them the way.

The burglar had certainly done his work thoroughly. Every scrap of paper the desk contained had apparently been examined, but he had left nothing behind to show why he had come or who he had been. There was a heap of charred paper in the grate, and squatting down Mr. Whipple examined this carefully.

The bulk of it was black and powdery, but there were two small pieces that had not been completely burned. One was indecipherable, but on the other it was possible to make out the word 'birthmark.' He showed this scrap to Gallers, but the inspector could make nothing of it.

'What do you think it is?' he asked.

Mr. Whipple shook his head.

'Really I — er — I wouldn't like to say,' he replied. 'It may be important, it may not.'

He put the little charred scrap carefully in an envelope and transferred it to his pocket. At present it conveyed nothing to him, but there was no knowing when it might prove very helpful indeed.

6

The Gelatine Circle

They went out and had a look round the neat garden. Going round to the small window by which the mysterious burglar had gained admission, they examined the sill and the ground beneath in the hope that it might yield something. The flower-bed was disturbed and there were marks of mud on the sill, but the marks were blurred and shapeless and as a means of identifying the shoes or boots which made them completely useless.

Re-entering the house, Mr. Whipple made a second examination of the disordered study, and this time he made a discovery. Stuck in a corner of the hearth was a little circular object that gleamed redly. Stooping, he discovered that it was a round wafer of coloured gelatine. Taking out his penknife he opened the blade, slipped it carefully beneath the sticky little mass and detached it from the tiles.

There was a faint, aromatic smell about it and he frowned at it for a long time, his face screwed up into a puzzled expression. Suddenly he gave an exclamation.

'Dear me!' he murmured. 'How very extraordinary! Yes, that is no doubt it.'

The little gelatine circle followed the charred scrap of paper and was stowed away in his pocket. Going out into the hall, he found Gallers talking to Marion.

'It's an extraordinary coincidence,' the girl was saying, 'that there should have been a burglary on the same night as — as — ' She stopped.

'Possibly it was not a coincidence at all,' said Mr. Whipple gently.

She looked at him.

'Do you mean that — that it is connected with my father's death?' she asked.

'Yes.' The little man nodded. 'Yes, I'm sure it was.'

'But there was nothing of any value in the desk,' she began.

'Not intrinsically, perhaps,' broke in Mr. Whipple. 'I think, however, there was something of value all the same. Tell me, Miss Rawlings, and forgive me for mentioning the matter, but did your father ever speak about the Rayden crime?'

'Oh yes, often,' she answered. 'It rather worried him. You know, it was the only case in which he was unsuccessful.'

Mr. Whipple nodded. 'Yes, I know that,' he answered, 'and I'm inclined to — er — believe — er — that it is at the bottom of this — er — recent terrible tragedy.'

She looked at him in surprise. 'I don't see how it could be,' she said softly. 'It happened so long ago. Besides, there was that letter.'

'All the same,' said Mr. Whipple deprecatingly, 'my theory is that the motive behind the — behind your father's death is connected with the murder of Mrs. Bedwell. Do you know if he had worked on the case at all since his retirement?'

'Oh yes, he had,' she answered at once. 'I know that. Not so very long ago, he was talking about it — I think it was a week or a fortnight ago — and he said he might have a surprise for them at the Yard very soon.'

'Dear me, he said that, did he?' said the little man, opening his eyes very wide behind his spectacles. 'Did he say anything else?'

She shook her head.

'No, father never discussed his cases with me,' she said. 'Not until they were all over.'

'So you don't know whether he had found anything definite or not?' asked Mr. Whipple.

'Not for certain,' she replied. 'But I think he had, from his manner. For the last few months he has been very busy indeed, and I think it must have been something to do with the murder at Rayden.'

'Was he — I'm sure you'll forgive all these questions, Miss Rawlings,' — Mr. Whipple was a little embarrassed — 'was he in the habit of making notes about these cases?'

'Sometimes,' said the girl, 'if he was dealing with one that was particularly intricate, but they were very scrappy.'

'I see,' murmured Mr. Whipple, nodding several times. 'Yes, I see. Now — er — with reference to this broadcast he was going to make. Did he show you the manuscript?'

'No,' she answered. 'I wanted to read it, but he wouldn't let me. He said that he would rather I listened in and heard it that way.'

He and Gallers took their leave a short while after, and on the way back to town Mr. Whipple was unusually silent. When they reached Scotland Yard and Gallers was about to bid him goodbye, he put forward his request.

'Would you — would you mind very much, Mr. Gallers,' he said diffidently, 'finding out where Lemming and Morrison are at the moment?'

Gallers stared at him.

'Yes, I'll do that,' he said.

'Thank you,' said Mr. Whipple gratefully. 'Thank you very much indeed. And when you've — er — discovered it, would you come with me to see them? I feel that — er — perhaps your presence would add — er — weight to anything I have to say.'

Gallers suppressed a smile. The idea of Mr. Whipple interviewing two crooks of the calibre of Arthur Lemming and Jake Morrison on his own struck him as funny. 'Yes, I'll do that, Mr. Whipple,' he said indulgently, and the little man was profuse in his thanks.

When he had taken leave of Gallers, he made his way slowly to Broadcasting House. Here, after a great deal of trouble, he succeeded in securing an interview with the Administrative Controller, and to that greatly worried man put a series of questions which changed his worried expression into one of bewilderment.

'What on earth do you want to know all that for, Mr. — er — Mr. Whipple?' he asked, when the little man had finished.

Mr. Whipple smiled.

'I am naturally of a curious disposition,' he answered, and took his departure.

* * *

The newspapers made a big splash of the killing at Broadcasting House. The profession of the victim and the unusual setting had given them something over which they could let themselves go — and they did!

Mr. Arthur Lemming read the account with interest while he breakfasted in his room royally on sausages and fried potatoes. He was a jovial, red-faced man, inclined to stoutness; and although this fatness had been considerably reduced during his sojourn at Pentonville, he had put on several pounds since his release some time previously.

He read the account of Rawlings' death without much emotion and tossed

170

the paper across to the little wizened man who shared his lodgings. 'Rawlings has got his,' he remarked cheerfully, and skilfully speared an enormous piece of sausage with his fork. 'It was comin' to 'im for a long time, and now 'e's got it.'

'Serves the beggar right!' grunted Jake Morrison. 'The perjurin' blighter! Remember that time 'e got up in the witness box and swore he'd seen me in Denby Street at 'alf-past two on a Tuesday?'

Lemming nodded sympathetically.

'Perjury, that's what it was!' continued his companion. 'It was a Wednesday!'

'Well 'e won't perjure no more!' said the stout man complacently, helping himself to another cup of tea. 'I'll bet there's a lot of people who'll be glad to read the papers this morning.'

In this he was right, for among the criminal classes Ex-Superintendent Rawlings had not been popular.

They had finished their late meal. Mr. Lemming was very fond of his bed, and after a long spell of rising with the dawn, was taking advantage of the unaccustomed luxury of getting up when he liked

— when the slatternly woman from whom they rented the room poked her head round the door and informed them that there were two men waiting to see them.

'Who are they?' demanded Mr. Lemming.

The woman shook her head. 'I don't know,' she answered.

'Well, find out!' snapped the stout man. 'I ain't seein' anybody until I knows who they are!'

'I think you'll see me, Lemming,' broke in a gruff voice, and Mr. Lemming's florid face went pale.

'Blimey, Gallers!' he exclaimed, and the inspector, who had followed the woman up the stairs, pushed past her and entered the room, accompanied by the small, insignificant figure of Mr. Whipple.

Mr. Lemming got to his feet rather clumsily. The unexpectedness of this visit had, for the moment, thrown him off his balance.

'Come in, Mr. Gallers,' he said, making a valiant effort to appear at his ease. 'Glad to see yer. Jake, get a chair for the gentleman.'

'I won't sit down, thanks,' said Gallers.

'I've just called in to have a chat with you, Lemming.'

The fat crook wiped the back of his hand across his mouth.

'Nothin' wrong, is there?' he asked anxiously. 'I mean, you 'aven't got anything on me, 'ave you? Me and Jake's going straight now — '

'Yes, I know all about that,' broke in the inspector.

Mr. Lemming looked at him with innocence all over his large face.

'It's the truth, I'm tellin' yer, Mr. Gallers,' he said. 'We 'ad our lesson over that bank job. We ain't goin' to get into no more trouble.'

'Not until the next time, I suppose,' said Gallers genially. 'You're not original, Lemming — they all say the same.'

He glanced round the shabby, untidy little room and his eyes lighted on the paper which Jake Morrison had thrown down at his entrance.

'I see you've been reading the news,' he said.

Mr. Lemming nodded.

'Very sad, ain't it, about poor Rawlings,'

he murmured mournfully. 'Nice feller 'e was, too. Too good for a blinkin' 'busy', I always said. I tell you, when I saw what 'ad 'appened to 'im it brought tears to me eyes!'

'I'm sure it did,' said Gallers sarcastically. 'Perhaps what I'm going to say will bring a few more. What part did you play in this murder?'

His last words were sharp and peremptory.

'Me?' Mr. Lemming's faded blue eyes opened wide. 'Why, nothin'! I wouldn't 'ave h'injured a 'air of 'is 'ead. Me and Rawlings was like brothers and — '

'What were you doing between seven-thirty and eight-thirty last night?' snapped the inspector.

For the first time a tinge of alarm crept into the face of the man opposite him.

'Look 'ere, what's the idea?' he demanded. 'You ain't tryin' to swing this killin' on us, are you?'

'That's not an answer to my question,' said Gallers, and he repeated it.

'Where was we, Jake?' said Mr. Lemming, wrinkling his brows.

'In the pub round the corner,' grunted Jake.

'Yes, I remembers now,' said the stout man. 'That's where we was. 'avin' a quiet drink with a few friends. They'll tell you the same if you asks them.'

'Your friends would say anything,' said Gallers. 'Look here, Lemming, I want the truth. You wrote a threatening letter to Rawlings a few days ago — '

'What's that?' broke in Mr. Lemming. 'Me write to Rawlings! Somebody's been kiddin' yer, Mr. Gallers. I wouldn't write to that feller. Why should I?'

'Are you telling me you didn't write to him?' said the inspector.

'Course I am!' broke in the other. 'We never wrote no letter, did we, Jake?'

Mr. Morrison shook his head.

'And as to threatening 'im,' continued Mr. Lemming indignantly, 'we wouldn't do such a thing. Neither me nor Jake bore Rawlings any malice. You know 'ow these things are, Mr. Gallers,' — his voice was ingratiating — 'thievin's just a game with two players, us and the perlice. If they snooker us, good luck to them. If we can

175

beat them, good luck to us. But we don't bear no malice, you know that as well as I do.'

Gallers did know this. Between the professional detective and the professional burglar there was no real ill feeling. As Lemming said, it was just a game in which the better player won.

'So you didn't write to Rawlings,' he said, 'reminding him of April the fourteenth, nineteen twenty-three, and threatening him?'

'No, I'll take me oath I didn't.' said Mr. Lemming earnestly. 'Wot's the date mean, any'ow?'

Gallers smiled.

'It was the date on which you and Morrison were sentenced for the National Union Bank affair,' he answered.

'Struth, so it was!' said Mr. Lemming in surprise. 'Fancy me not remembering that!'

Watching him keenly, Mr. Whipple was convinced the man was speaking the truth. He had forgotten the date, in which case he had not written that letter which Rawlings had received two days before his death. This fitted in with the little man's preconceived theory.

'Do you — do you know a Mr. Lew Shale?' he asked timidly, and Mr. Lemming smiled.

'I used ter know 'im,' he answered. ' 'E's gone out of the business now — same as we 'ave,' he added hastily. 'Playing the saxophone or something in some band. 'e was always musical.'

'When — when did you last see him?' said Mr. Whipple.

The stout man's forehead puckered.

'Lemme see now,' he muttered. 'When did we last see Lew, Jake?'

The wizened little man scratched his head.

'Not since three months ago,' he answered. 'Don't you remember, we ran into 'im in that pub off Shaftesbury Avenue.'

'Yes, that's right,' said Mr. Lemming, 'and 'e told us 'e was givin' up the game and runnin' straight. Very glad I was to 'ear it, too,' he added virtuously. 'Honesty is the best policy, after all.'

'What are you doing now?' asked Gallers, and Mr. Lemming became suddenly confused.

'Just lookin' around,' he began vaguely. 'We've got one or two jobs in view — nothin' wrong. We wouldn't do anythin' like that now.'

'Why try to fool me?' said the inspector. 'I know you, Lemming, and I know Morrison. Neither of you could even fall straight.'

They united in their protestations. A few seconds later Gallers and Mr. Whipple took their leave.

'Well,' said the inspector, 'I hope you've learned what you wanted to know.'

'Yes, thank you,' said Mr. Whipple, and leaving his friend he went blithely back home.

He spent the rest of the day indoors; and during the evening Gallers, dropping in to see him, found him busily engaged at his desk. When he saw the half-dozen or so slips of paper neatly ruled into squares, he raised his eyebrows.

'What on earth are you doing, Mr. Whipple?' he asked.

Mr. Whipple looked up with a gentle smile.

'Making up a crossword puzzle,' he replied.

'I can see that,' said Gallers. 'But why? I didn't know you went in for this sort of thing.'

'I don't as a rule,' confessed the little man, 'but I think it's going to help in solving the mystery of Rawlings' murder.'

7

Mr. Whipple Gets Busy

During the two days that followed, Mr. Whipple was a very busy man indeed. A great part of his time was spent at Broadcasting House, chatting nervously to the various officials of the B.B.C. He had a long interview with the man in charge of the filing room, and also the head of the talk department, whose duty it was to read and correct all manuscripts before they were broadcast. He spent several hours with this pleasant gentleman, who was immensely interested in the mystery surrounding the death of ex-Superintendent Rawlings.

'I remember quite a lot of the talk,' he

said, in answer to Mr. Whipple's question. 'A great part simply recapitulated the murder at Rayden and the investigations that Rawlings conducted at the time. But I can't remember anything that is likely to help you, I'm afraid.'

'Did — er — did Rawlings offer anything in the nature of a solution to the mystery?' asked Mr. Whipple.

The Director of Talk shook his head.

'Not that I can remember,' he said. 'As a matter of fact criminology is not a hobby of mine, otherwise I might have taken more interest. I remember the Rayden case, of course, but only vaguely. The dead woman had a son or something, hadn't she?'

'Dear me, not that I am aware of,' said Mr. Whipple, and the other shrugged his shoulders.

'I must have made a mistake,' he replied. 'Yet I could have sworn I remembered something about a son being mentioned in connection with her.'

'The only place you could have seen that mentioned,' said Mr. Whipple slowly, 'was in Rawlings' manuscript.'

The head of the Talk Department frowned.

'Maybe that's where it was,' he answered. 'But I couldn't be certain. I have to read a tremendous number of manuscripts,' he added, as an excuse for his bad memory.

'Do you — do you remember anything about a birthmark?' asked Mr. Whipple, and the other pursed up his lips and scratched gently at his chin.

'Now you remind me,' he said, 'I believe there was something — yes, there was.'

Mr. Whipple's eyes gleamed behind his glasses.

'Was — was the birthmark in connection with this alleged son of the dead woman's?' he asked.

The Talk Director wrinkled his brows and it was a long time before he answered.

'I'm sorry,' he confessed at last, 'But I really can't tell you. I believe there was something about a son mentioned, and I'm sure there was something about a birthmark, but I can't say any more than that.'

Mr. Whipple felt a little disappointed. It

was certain that in these two words lay the vital part of Rawlings' manuscript — the part that had made it essential for somebody to prevent its being broadcast. He had recently studied all the available data concerning the Rayden crime, and in none of the newspaper reports or other documents that he had examined had there been any mention of a son or a birthmark. If either of these things had been contained in the manuscript of Rawlings' talk, then both of them must have referred to something that the superintendent had discovered during his later investigations into the Bedwell murder.

He tried his best to jog the Talk Director's memory, but without result, and was forced at last, rather disappointedly, to take his leave. He felt certain that here was a clue that just eluded his grasp. If only it were possible to know for certain what Rawlings had been going to say. Everything in connection with that talk of his had been destroyed. The heap of burnt paper in the grate of the house at Highgate had obviously been his rough notes from which the manuscript had been compiled, and they were a mass of burnt ash — with the exception of that one word which he had managed to extract from the debris.

He left the Talk Department and went slowly upstairs to the office of the Administrative Controller.

'Sit down,' said Major Marshland resignedly. He was getting a little tired of Mr. Whipple.

'Thank you, thank you very much,' said the little man. 'But if you'll excuse me, I'm rather in a hurry. Did you get those things I asked for?'

The Administrative Controller nodded, opened a drawer in his desk and took out an envelope.

'Yes, here you are,' he said, handing it over, 'though what in the world you've got in the back of your mind is a mystery to me.'

'If I'm at all lucky,' said Mr. Whipple, 'it won't be for long,' and he took his departure.

From Broadcasting House he went to Southampton Row, and entered a block of buildings containing the laboratory of an analytical chemist. When he finally left to make his way home, his face wore an expression of satisfaction.

Gallers, who was immensely interested in the activities of his little neighbour, came in during the evening and found him examining a half-dozen slips of paper.

'Hello!' he said. 'Still doing crosswords, Mr. Whipple?'

'Er — yes,' said Mr. Whipple, continuing his task.

'That fellow Shale is being formally charged tomorrow,' said the inspector.

Mr. Whipple looked up with a troubled expression on his face.

'I really think it ought to be prevented,' he said. 'Couldn't you — couldn't you possibly suggest to Inspector Harris to — er — to delay matters for a little while? Only a day — '

Gallers looked at him quickly.

'I believe you know something,' he grunted.

'No, really, I — I know nothing definite,' declared Mr. Whipple. 'But I've got a — er a theory and I think I can

— er — prove it tonight.'

He leaned forward and for the next half hour began to speak rapidly and nervously, and Gallers' eyes opened wider and wider as he proceeded.

8

The Birthmark

The evening programmes at Broadcasting House were nearing an end. In the studio allotted for the purpose, the B.B.C. Dance Orchestra were awaiting the flicker of the red light that warned them to begin their signature tune. In the Balance and Control Room they were waiting for the last news to finish before fading in the dance music. In his office on the second floor Mr. Gilmour, the House Superintendent, was initialing a batch of the day's reports. In his studio on the seventh floor James Henley was finishing reading the last General News Bulletin for that day. In his office on the sixth floor Mr. McGrath, the Studio Manager, was smoking a cigarette and staring fixedly at nothing, his shaggy brows drawn together in a frown. In the listening room on the seventh floor Detective-Inspector Harris, Gallers, and two plain-clothes men were listening to the conclusion of a military band concert from the Midland Studio. And in his ultra-modern office the Administrative Controller, Major Marshland, was sitting at his desk reading for the sixth time the letter which had reached him earlier that evening.

James Henley came to the last item of news:

'That is the end of the second General News Bulletin. The London, Scottish and Midland Regionals are closing down. There will be dance music from the National transmitter until midnight. Good night everyone — Good night!'

He sat back in his chair and waited until the red light went out, then with a sigh of relief he collected up the papers on which were typed the various news items that he had been reading. The day was nearly over and he was glad.

He came out of the studio, shut the

door behind him, and pausing in the corridor lit a cigarette. He heard the whine of an ascending lift; presently the grill opened and a pageboy came towards him.

'Major Marshland wants you to go to his office at once, sir,' said the messenger.

Henley frowned. He was tired, longing to get home to his flat and sleep, but an order was an order and it had to be obeyed.

He went down in the lift and made his way to the Administrative Controller's office. The big room was brilliantly lit: all the concealed cornice lamps were turned on, and he was surprised to find that Marshland was not alone. With him was Gilmour, the House Superintendent; McGrath, the Studio Manager; Hillard, the Chief Announcer; Detective-Inspector Harris; Gallers; two other men who were obviously plain-clothes policemen; and the small figure of Mr. Whipple. There was another man whom he recognised with surprise as the manager of the Filing Department.

The Administrative Controller, a worried frown creasing his forehead, looked up as he entered.

'Come in, Henley,' he said, 'and sit down. I've called this conference here tonight at the request of Detective-Inspector Harris. Mr. — er — Mr. Whipple has, I believe, something to say with regard to the murder of ex-Superintendent Rawlings.'

Henley found a chair and seated himself.

'I think everyone you mentioned is present,' went on Marshland, looking at the little man.

Mr. Whipple's eyes travelled slowly round the room and he nodded.

'I — I'm very sorry,' he began apologetically, 'to have brought you all here at such a late hour. I've no doubt that the majority of you are tired after your long day's work and looking forward to going home. I — I sincerely hope that it will not be necessary to keep you very long. I'll try and — er — say what I have to say as briefly as possible.'

He cleared his throat.

'The tragedy which happened in this building and which forms the reason for my having asked Major Marshland to call you here tonight,' he continued, 'is still fresh in your memory, and therefore there is no need for me to — to go over its circumstances. You all know that ex-Superintendent Rawlings was shot at the beginning of his talk on the Rayden murder case in studio sixteen. What you do not know is who shot him and why. In the course of the next few minutes I — I hope to be able to tell you.'

A little murmur of surprise ran round the group who were listening to him, but Mr. Whipple took no notice and went on almost directly:

'There were several people who could have done it,' he said. 'Lew Shale, the man who has been arrested. Mr. McGrath, the Studio Manager, who had no alibi for that time. Mr. Gilmour, the House Superintendent, who also had no alibi. Mr. Hillard, the Chief Announcer, or Mr. Henley. Any one of the persons I have mentioned could have killed Rawlings and — and one of them did, as you will presently see. Before I — I go any further I may as well state that the murderer is in this room. It would save a great amount of time if he would step forward and — and confess to the crime.'

He paused, his eyes moving from face to face, but no one moved. The faces before him were pale and strained, and into the atmosphere of the brilliantly lit office had crept a tenseness — the tenseness that settles over a theatre at the moment before the curtain rises.

'I — I made the suggestion,' went on Mr. Whipple, still in his nervous apologetic way, 'without very much hope that it would be acted upon. However, it is immaterial, for I know which of you shot Rawlings down at the microphone in the studio before he could broadcast his talk on the Rayden murder.'

Somebody drew in their breath sharply, and Marshland moved uneasily in his padded chair.

'I — I may as well begin,' continued Mr. Whipple, 'with the motive, and from the first this seemed very obvious. The time at which the murder was committed, the fact that every manuscript of the talk was missing, and that someone had — er — even taken the trouble to pay a midnight visit to the superintendent's house and destroy the notes he had made, clearly pointed to the fact that it was one of those cases in which a second crime had to be committed in order to cover up another. The subject of the talk proved, without doubt, what that other crime was. Some years ago an old woman was strangled in her house in Rayden. The murderer was never discovered and it was one of the few failures which Superintendent Rawlings, who was in charge of the case, had against him. After he retired he worked steadily to wipe out this failure and, I believe, he succeeded. He discovered a clue which he rightly concluded would lead to the capture of the Rayden murderer. He found out that Mrs. Bedwell had a son and that the son bore a birthmark in the rough shape of a rat.'

Again a little murmur came from the people listening.

'He kept this discovery to himself,' said Mr. Whipple. 'He had no idea of the name or the identity of the man who bore this mark, and the task of running him to earth was almost colossal. Then he was invited by the B.B.C. to contribute to the series of talks on unsolved crimes. It was suggested that he should base his talk on the Rayden murder. Immediately he saw the chance that presented itself. If, in the course of his talk, he mentioned the fact that the murderer bore this certain mark, there was just a possibility that someone among his listeners would remember having seen such a mark on one of their friends or acquaintances and communicate with him. Unfortunately he was — er — killed before he could carry out his intentions.

'Obviously the murder could only have been committed by someone connected with the B.B.C. No stranger could have penetrated to studio number sixteen, neither would he have taken the risk of waiting until Rawlings had actually started his talk before shooting him. Again, it could only have been a member of the staff who knew what his talk contained — someone who had read the manuscript.

'This narrowed things down considerably; and the letter which Rawlings received before the broadcast purporting to come from Lemming and Morrison, threatening his life, narrowed things down still more. In fact, it supplied the final proof of the identity of the person who killed Rawlings.'

Mr. Whipple paused and moistened his lips. The people before him were staring fixedly with set faces, but no one spoke.

'The letter was in printed characters written in pencil,' the little man went on, his nervousness decreasing as he continued. 'Inspector Gallers, at my request, interviewed both Lemming and Morrison, taking me with him, and I came to the conclusion that it was a blind. Without telling Major Marshland my reasons, I arranged with him to circulate among his staff a — a crossword puzzle, which I myself made up and which introduced three of the words in the threatening letter.

'As you know, people always fill in crosswords with capitals. I have the filled-in puzzles here.' He drew an envelope from his breast pocket.

'One of them corresponds exactly with the writing of the threatening letter. That was the murderer's first mistake. His — second was when he spat out a throat lozenge in the grate of Rawlings' house at Highgate. I found it and — er — had it analysed. It — it was a brand known as 'Clarabel', and from Major Marshland I learned that there was one member of his staff who habitually sucked these lozenges. He is the man who — who bought the toy pistol, filed off the end of the barrel and shot Rawlings; the man who strangled Mrs. Bedwell at Rayden; the man who has on his body a — er — birthmark in the shape of a rat and — '

There was a sudden movement among his audience.

'Look out, Harris!' cried Gallers sharply, as Henley, his face distorted, sprang to his feet.

The inspector, who had been standing close to him, swung round and gripped him by the arm. Henley's left shot out and caught him full on the point of the chin. With a gasp Harris staggered backwards, cannoning into the two plain-clothes men who were moving forward to his assistance.

With a bound Henley reached the door, and before anyone could stop him had jerked it open and disappeared into the corridor. With his heart beating furiously, he raced to the vestibule. A pattering of steps came from behind him and as he reached the circular entrance to the hall he looked back. Gallers and the two detectives were hot on his heels. He turned towards the swing doors and stopped like a trapped animal. Two other men were stationed there, obviously policemen; and as they caught sight of him they came towards him. His brain worked rapidly. It was useless fighting — this was the end — but he wouldn't be hanged, anyway.

He swung round, eluded Gallers's outstretched hand and dashed towards a narrow door on the opposite side. Bursting through it, he clattered down a flight of stone steps with his pursuers close behind him. The steady hum of machinery came to his ears, and running along a brightly lit corridor he came to his objective — the machine room.

A row of humming dynamos supplying

the light and power to Broadcasting House was on his left. Without hesitation he rushed to the nearest one; and as Gallers and the plain-clothes men flung themselves through the doorway, he leaped onto the concrete base and grasped the shining terminals.

A spark of blue flame hissed viciously. A mechanic uttered a cry and pulled frantically at a big switch. The figure of Henley crumpled, sagged to its knees, and rolling off the concrete base lay still upon the stone floor.

⋆　⋆　⋆

The action of the engineer in pulling out the switch saved Henley's life temporarily, and he lived for thirty-six hours after his attempted suicide. During the one period of consciousness that came just before the end, he cleared up the last mystery surrounding the Rayden crime.

Mrs. Bedwell in her youth had been the housekeeper to a wealthy nobleman. During this period a child had been born, and that child was James Henley. His mother had always hated him; at an early age he was sent to boarding school and was not allowed even to see her during the holidays. A few years later his father, Lord — , had married. Mrs. Bedwell had taken advantage of this fact to levy blackmail. Regularly every quarter, she received the sum of three hundred pounds in cash. She was suspicious of banks; and being of a miserly disposition, she saved the greater part of this, keeping it in a steel box beneath her bed.

She had, almost from the time Henley reached boyhood, refused to acknowledge her son or have anything to do with him, and Henley's early life had been one continual fight against starvation. He had slept on the Embankment, been a sandwich-board man, sold matches in the gutter and in various ways scraped together a precarious livelihood.

For years he had lost sight of his mother altogether, and then had come the war. The army, after his previous exist-ence, was Heaven. Here at least he had warm clothing and food. His education had been a good one and he quickly rose from the ranks. When the Armistice was signed he was Major James Henley, of the Sixteenth Berkshire Fusiliers. He received a small pension, but his life in the army had taught him extravagance and he quickly found that this was not nearly enough to satisfy his luxurious ideas of living. He tried various jobs, but as fast as he got out of one scrape his extravagance led him into another, until a few years after he had been demobilised there were writs out against him on all sides and he had to disappear to hide from his creditors.

Knowing that his mother was in receipt of a substantial quarterly sum from his father, he tried to find her, and eventually succeeded in doing so. He was completely down on his uppers by this time, and when he tried to get her to help him she refused to have anything to do with him.

Her death at Rayden had been more of an accident than anything else. He had, some years before, converted his pension into a lump sum in order to start a business, which had failed; and when he came that evening to the little house in Rayden he was penniless and starving.

His mother had tried to close the door in his face but he had forced his way in. He had no intention of doing any violence, but the old woman had goaded him into a fury, and before he quite knew what had happened he had strangled her. He was horror-stricken; but now that he had done it he decided that he was not going away empty-handed.

He found a key on a chain round her neck and discovered that it fitted a steel box under the bed. When he opened it he found a little over two thousand pounds in notes. With this windfall he was able to make himself respectable, buy new clothes and decent food, and live comfortably until such time as he could find a job which would augment his capital.

He was a long time looking round, and the two thousand was nearly gone before he eventually managed to secure a position as an announcer at the B.B.C. To do this he had to forge university references.

A year later he married and settled down to what he hoped would be a peaceful life. Then came Rawlings' broadcast talk and the bombshell that threatened to destroy him. How the ex-superintendent had found out that Mrs. Bedwell had a son and that the son bore a birthmark in the shape of a rat was a mystery to Henley; but if that talk was broadcast, and Diana, his young wife, heard the description of that mark, she would realize that she was married to a murderer.

It was to prevent his wife hearing, more than anything else, that he decided to kill Rawlings before he could send out to the world that fatal theory of the Rayden murder.

He had planned everything carefully. In the back files of a paper in Fleet Street he had read up on all the cases with which Rawlings had been connected, and in the National Union Bank robbery he had found what he was seeking. By careful inquiries he had found that Arthur Lemming and Jake Morrison had been released from prison, and wrote his threat to the man he had decided to kill. He guessed that the date would be sufficient to connect the bank robbers with the threatening letter.

He had meant to shoot Rawlings before his talk began — had based all his plans on this — but the Chief Announcer calling him away to send out the police message had made his first idea impossible. He had come back after making his preliminary announcement and shot the ex-superintendent while the microphone was live. He had already stolen the manuscript from the filing room and had only to throw down the pistol and collect the manuscript from under the dead body and hurry back to his own studio at the end of the corridor.

His statement was taken down by a shorthand writer in the presence of Inspector Harris and Inspector Gallers. Ten minutes after he had signed it, Henley was dead.

'Well, Mr. Whipple,' commented Mr. Gallers over a whisky and soda in the little man's study that evening, 'it was a neat piece of work. Poor Rawlings! He was a funny chap and personally I didn't get on with him very well, but it's dreadful that he should have gone out like that.'

Mr. Whipple nodded sympathetically.

'There are two people, I think,' he murmured diffidently, 'who — who deserve more sympathy: ex-superintendent Rawlings' daughter and Henley's wife. It's a great deal harder to live than die, don't you think so, Mr. Gallers?'

THE END

Books by Gerald Verner
in the Linford Mystery Library:

THE LAST WARNING
DENE OF THE SECRET SERVICE
THE NURSERY RHYME MURDERS
TERROR TOWER
THE CLEVERNESS OF MR. BUDD
THE SEVEN LAMPS
THEY WALK IN DARKNESS
THE HEEL OF ACHILLES
DEAD SECRET
MR. BUDD STEPS IN
THE RETURN OF MR. BUDD
MR. BUDD AGAIN
QUEER FACE
THE CRIMSON RAMBLERS
GHOST HOUSE
THE ANGEL
DEATH SET IN DIAMONDS
THE CLUE OF THE GREEN CANDLE
THE 'Q' SQUAD
MR. BUDD INVESTIGATES
THE RIVER HOUSE MYSTERY
NOOSE FOR A LADY

THE FACELESS ONES
GRIM DEATH
MURDER IN MANUSCRIPT
THE GLASS ARROW
THE THIRD KEY
THE ROYAL FLUSH MURDERS
THE SQUEALER
MR. WHIPPLE EXPLAINS
THE SEVEN CLUES

We do hope that you have enjoyed reading this large print book.

Did you know that all of our titles are available for purchase?

We publish a wide range of high quality large print books including:
Romances, Mysteries, Classics
General Fiction
Non Fiction and Westerns

Special interest titles available in large print are:
The Little Oxford Dictionary
Music Book, Song Book
Hymn Book, Service Book

Also available from us courtesy of Oxford University Press:
Young Readers' Dictionary
(large print edition)
Young Readers' Thesaurus
(large print edition)

For further information or a free brochure, please contact us at:
Ulverscroft Large Print Books Ltd.,
The Green, Bradgate Road, Anstey,
Leicester, LE7 7FU, England.
Tel: (00 44) **0116 236 4325**
Fax: (00 44) **0116 234 0205**

WREATH FOR A LADY

John Glasby

When Mike Torlin takes on the job of investigating the strange happenings at Pete Donati's carnival ground, he figures it's a straightforward case of somebody wanting to put Donati out of business. Then a peculiar chicken is produced out of an egg: a dead girl, shot with slugs from her own shooting gallery. No killer can sidetrack Mike Torlin for long and get away with it — and when the final showdown comes, he is forced to stand his ground and face up to the killer . . .

MORTAL PROSE

Geraldine Ryan

When a mogul of the literary world is murdered, D.I. Casey Clunes is on the case — though the victim's unpopularity ensures no shortage of suspects ... Isobel is an intelligent woman ... except when it comes to her new toyboy. Still, their relationship couldn't harm anyone else — or could it ... ? The audience gasps as the new portrait of the headmaster of St Martin's is publicly revealed — defaced — followed by news that the headmaster himself has been shot dead by an unknown assailant ... Three stories of mystery and murder from the pen of Geraldine Ryan.

A CORNISH REVENGE

Rena George

A bleak Cornish clifftop strewn with the derelict remains of old tin mines seems to magazine editor Loveday Ross an odd place for an art class; her artist friend Lawrence Kemp has been acting strangely recently. As Loveday takes the pictures she needs for an article, a grim sight emerges as the tide recedes below. It's the body of a man who, Loveday realises with horror, was deliberately left to drown. But why has the discovery, awful though it is, affected Lawrence and his students so deeply?

BABY BOY BLUE

Marilyn Brahen

In 1944, young Walter Buehl finds his mother stabbed to death on the kitchen floor and his teenage brother Tony crouching beside her, bloody knife in hand. Forty-one years later, Tony escapes from a psychiatric hospital, and a series of murders ensues — with Tony as the main suspect. But Lieutenant Asher Lowenstein isn't convinced of Tony's guilt, and he asks his friend, psychic Tam Westington, to help. As the police conduct a manhunt for the Baby Boy Blue killer, a long-buried truth may surface — at the cost of more lives . . .

BLOOD LINES

Catriona McCuaig

Post-war midwife Maudie Rouse has her hands full tending to the pregnant, sick and injured villagers of Llandy-fan, acting as their counsellor, and preparing for changes as the NHS comes into existence — including the possibility of being forced to move away from the people and the job she loves. The call of duty is never far away, even when she tries to steal a private moment with Constable Dick Bryant. Then a fortune-teller is found murdered at the village fête, and Maudie and Dick team up to search for answers . . .